Other Books by C.S. Humble

THE BLACK WELLS SERIES
Via Dark Hart Books

BOOK 1 - **ALL THESE SUBTLE DECEITS** (2022)

BOOK 2 - **ALL THE PROSPECT AROUND US** (2022)

BOOK 3 - **ALL THAT MANKIND FAILS TO BEAR** (2024)

THAT LIGHT SUBLIME TRILOGY
Via Cemetery Dance

BOOK 1 - **THE MASSACRE AT YELLOW HILL**

BOOK 2 - **A RED WINTER IN THE WEST** (JULY, 2023)

BOOK 3 - **THE LIGHT OF A BLACK STAR** (NOVEMBER, 2023)

Note From the Author

This version of the novel is a revised edition that has removed racial epithets which were included in the novel's original printing in 2018. At the time of the book's first publication, I believed that the historicity of the language used by racists was important to the novel's direct characterization of racists and the terms they used. However, my position on the matter changed to a more educated and, what I believe to be, a more just approach to persons of color and a greater understanding of the trauma those terms cause in their lives.

This does not excuse the inclusion of those
terms in the original publication.
It only seeks to rectify that mistake.

— C.S. Humble, 2021

The Massacre
at Yellow Hill

The Massacre at Yellow Hill

THAT LIGHT SUBLIME TRILOGY

Book One

C.S. Humble

CEMETERY DANCE PUBLICATIONS

Baltimore

2023

Cemetery Dance Publications
132B Industry Lane, Unit #7
Forest Hill, MD 21050
www.cemeterydance.com

Trade Paperback Edition

ISBN:
978-1-58767-891-2

Part I:
THE WIDOW AND HER CHILDREN

&

Part II:
PTOLEMY AND SON

&

Part III:
THE MASSACRE AT YELLOW HILL

Dedicated to Rob and Brad

Uva Uvam Videndo Varia Fit

Last eve the sunset winds upheaved
A mountain in the west,
All seamed with gloomy gulfs, from base
Up to its golden crest;
Cloud piled on cloud that mountain rose—
A storm whose wrath was spent—
Its routed legions gathered up,
In common ruin blent;
And all about its dark base rolled
A sea of gorgeous dyes,
And on its summit blazed a fire
Too bright for mortal eyes;
And grandly down its southern slope
A purpling river flowed
Into the sea of gorgeous dyes
Which at its foot abode.

— M.H. Cobb, *The Mountain in the West*

Part I:

THE WIDOW AND HER CHILDREN

Chapter One

YELLOW HILL, TEXAS

JEREMIAH HART STOOD over the body, tracing his eyes over long crimson valleys. The deep punctures along the man's shoulder expanded down the stomach into ragged lines where a bulbous sack and purple intestines spilled out onto the parlor table.

Hart let out a low hum through the folds of his frown. He closed his eyes. The well-greased cogs of his mind were spinning. His eyes opened, and he used them like a hammer, striking the three men who stood with wide-brimmed hats in hands, studying their boots on the opposite side of what was left of George Miller.

"Foreman," Hart said.

"Yes, sir." Charlie Gathers clenched every hole south of his belt. His knee was all twisted up and swollen. He'd felt some kind of heavy pop in the joint while pulling George from the mine. That didn't matter now though. What mattered was that Hart wasn't happy. Jobs would get cut and heads would roll with them. Please just fire me and let me go home, he thought.

"First question." His voice flat and hard as a penny. "Why did you bring this man's body out of the mine without consulting me or Sheriff Baily?"

Charlie looked at Lucas Ramos to his right. The Mexican stared at his boot tips, silent. He swung his head left to Mark Marple, who slumped at the shoulders, his hands behind the hat he held.

"Foreman?" Hart said.

Charlie's head quaked, "I, uh—well, sir." He swallowed hard. "George here was still screaming when we was pullin' him out. He didn't stop hollering until we'd jerked him out of the shaft. And it—it's so dark down there, I don't think anyone saw how bad it was until we got him out into the light."

"I did," Lucas said.

"The *hell* you did. You couldn't see shit," Charlie cut in.

Lucas shuffled his boots on the floor of Doc Carte's parlor, then said, "I did, boss. George was trying to stuff his guts back into his belly."

"Whatever he thought he saw, Mr. Hart," Charlie snapped, "the point is, George Miller was still alive after Mark here scared the thing off with his revolver. I just didn't think it proper to leave a wounded man—"

"Didn't think it proper," Hart said.

Charlie wilted at the words.

"You jeopardized the entire operation. Months of work and tens of thousands of dollars pissed away because you were worried about, what? Propriety? Your fucking manners?" Hart let the rebuke hang in the air. "You are the foreman. If you had the sense God gave a mule, you'd have left Miller at the teeth of this so-called wolf. Even a damn idiot knows a man with his belly spilled open is a lost cause. You should have been securing the mine's safety. Instead,

The Massacre at Yellow Hill

you stumbled out of the main shaft, breaking several lamps, which burned half a dozen men trying to get out behind you."

"Mister Hart—"

"*Subsequently*," Hart said, his voice rising, "the fire caught a gas pocket"—he was screaming now—"causing an explosion that caved-in a third of our fucking progress!"

Charlie shook his head, unsure of himself. Unsure of what to say. "I just reacted, Mr. Hart."

"I don't pay men to react, foreman. I pay some to dig, and some to build, and one—just one fucking man out of a hundred—I pay to think, so that the others will have a singular voice of thoughtful command when things go to shit."

"I'm sorry, Mr. Hart."

"Charlie, your uncle was one of the best men I ever knew. In the ten years he served as my foreman, not one single motherfucking problem darkened our progress," Hart said.

Charlie knew neither of those things were true.

"You've been foreman for three months, and now here, at my very goddamn feet I have a dead man, a whole mess of others burned to a crisp, and two months of work lost. And all you have to tell me is some bullshit story about seeing a wolf hiding in the mine? Whereupon, instead of acting like men, you all shit your britches and caused the biggest mining catastrophe since—No, not since; it's the worst of all time. The worst fucking operating tragedy in the *history of Yellow Hill.*"

And then, surprising all in the room, including himself, Charlie said, "All due respect, Mr. Hart, but it weren't no damn wolf in the mine. The boys who didn't see what happened, they called it a wolf, and I'm sure that's why you're doing it too. But that ain't what it was, sir. That ain't what it was at all."

Hart's mouth hung open, tongue gliding over molars, furious.

"I grew up on a sheep farm, Mr. Hart," Charlie continued, "and, sir, I know what a wolf looks like in the dark. Hell, I know what it sounds like and how it acts. They don't hunt inside of mines, they aren't that damn big, and they sure as shit don't do this to people."

Hart lowered his voice. "You do not want to be taking that tone with me." The soft, almost gentle tone beveled the edge of the warning.

Charlie's brashness died a slow death in long, quiet space after those words.

Having cowed Charlie again, Hart offered, "A bear then. Call it a bear."

A bear? Charlie thought. *There's not a chance in hell…*

Mark Marple finally spoke up: "I don't reckon it a bear, sir."

Hart squinted at Mark. "A bar. A bar? What kind of accent is that?"

Charlie opened his mouth to answer.

"Wait," Hart said. "I don't give a shit." He pointed a hard finger at Mark. "Keep your mouth shut until you can learn to bend that German or Polish or whatever-the-fuck accent that is into something I can understand."

Mark submitted, his eyes cowing to the baseboards.

"Foreman, you take these two men, you cover this body in a tarp, and you take it out back to the barn. Then you go to the smith's shop and borrow a few hammers. Say it's for rock busting."

Hart leaned forward, pressing his weight into the table. His knuckles creased white. "Then you bust this man up until he looks like he was killed in the cave-in. If I hear anything about a bear or a wolf, it'll be the three of you trying to swim in the river of shit that'll follow."

The Massacre at Yellow Hill

Charlie shook his head, confused. "Why are we gonna lie about it?"

The wood groaned beneath Hart's knuckles. "Because I said so."

The small courage in Charlie shrank under Hart's glare.

"Now, you go get those hammers, and do like I say."

Hart walked over to the coat rack. "And, Charlie," he said, pulling his coat on, "when you're finished, you go over to the Miller place and explain—in stark, easily remembered detail—how their husband and father was killed in by a cave-in under your watch. Then tell the newly made widow that, as recompense, if she has a son worth his salt, I'll hire him at half his father's wages."

"That's awful neighborly of you, sir," Mark said.

"I always try to be fair, men."

"George's son can't be older than ten, Mr. Hart," Charlie said. "He can't work for a wage yet."

Hart jerked his coat straight. "Well, let them figure out their own trouble," he said. "If that wife of George Miller doesn't have a trade, we've always got the brothel."

Chapter Two

YELLOW HILL, TEXAS

THROUGH THE KITCHEN window, Tabitha Miller looked out onto a bruised dawn. Clouds, long and thin, stretched like a field of white reeds. The sun bulged over the horizon red and angry, lording over all creation. The stove fire made the heat even worse. She fanned herself and turned back to the eggs. Chewing her lip, wondering how to make it all last. The funeral cost almost the entire amount of George Miller's remaining wages. Mr. Hart shorted those wages under the pretense that they were 'prorated,' on the grounds George had died during the middle of the work week.

Wages that had barely covered weekly expenses were now gone completely, leaving Tabitha Miller uncertain how she would feed her family once the town's charity ran thin.

The Methodists gathered a love offering for her family, but these were mostly people who didn't have two nickels to rub together, so there was more love than offering.

The church gave what it had, but Tabitha knew it wouldn't last long, what with the cost of flour and beef being so high. There was the rent to consider, too. Hart owned the property, of course, and it lit a fire inside of her to know she was effectively returning the money Hart had paid for her husband's sweat and toil back to him.

Everything is discounted to the rich, she thought.

George's credit was all loaned out, though the bank hadn't the gall to ask for payment. Not yet, anyway. But Tabitha knew that once the cloud of tragedy passed, people would want their money, and they wouldn't care for anything else.

She had a sister in Colorado, but there was no amount of goodwill or charity in the town to spend on a widow and her two children's passage through hostile country with the likelihood being that they'd either perish on the trip or never earn enough to pay them back.

Yellow Hill was a hard place, sunbaked and sandy, giving very little to those who had struck out to find wealth on the frontier. It gave wealth in the hundreds of thousands to those who had money enough to buy land but offered only a daily wage for the unlucky and desperate men who now cowboyed for ranchers or swung pickaxes in the mine.

The mine was an endeavor wholly unique to Yellow Hill. No other town this far west in Texas had hacked into the skin of the world to look for gold, iron, or silver. Everyone Tabitha knew was of the opinion that Hart was a fool to waste his money on the operation. She'd mentioned that gossip to George only a few weeks before his death, but he told her that they weren't looking for veins of silver or gold but for some green river of shining crystal in the rock, though Hart never named the mineral outright.

George had signed on with Hart's company after finding most of the ranching jobs were taken and his attempt to become a farmer proved a bust. He'd been a man with a big arms and hands, and a

The Massacre at Yellow Hill

heart bigger still, but nothing about him proved capable in growing things. The first few crops were fine enough, even making a little money, but when the first drought hit, it was all over.

It was her last bit of inheritance George had spent on the doomed plot. Tabitha's mother and father had died during Sherman's raid into Georgia. Her family, even though they were abolitionists, saw their home burned, their holdings ravaged in the black line he burned through the state. The land of Yellow Hill had been cheap then, advertised as a land of promise. George had bought into the plot and the lie, moving them to West Texas.

Her sister Martha was now the only living relative she had not given birth to, and Tabitha had considered calling on her for help. Perhaps even to impose, travel to Denver where Martha lived in the desperate hope to start over.

Even if a miracle managed to get her and the children to Colorado, she couldn't be confident her sister would accept them. Martha Perrywell had married a gambler, despite their father's wishes, and Tabitha would be damned if she was going to uproot her children, despite their financial hardship, only to take them through Indian country into the home of a huckster. "Never trust a gambler or a politician," her father had said. "They both play the same perilous game. One with cards, the other with lives."

The sun was cresting over the rolling dunes as she made breakfast for the children, cracking a single egg for each of them, careful not to break the yolks in the hot iron skillet. She trimmed a slim piece of apple bread off the loaf that had come with the church's love offering. They couldn't afford bacon now, but the bacon had always been more for George than for Annie or Georgie. She, herself, would just manage with just coffee for now. The last egg would be her lunch.

At the table, Annie, her face still flushed and shiny from crying, poked the blue tin plate with her fork. Sitting beside her on the bench, little Georgie leaned on the table, sleeping atop his folded arms. The boy had often crawled into bed next to his father, but since the cave-in, the child found no rest without his father's warm comfort to help carry him off into dreams. Tabitha held him close during the night, but her son just rolled over and over in constant agitation. Even when Georgie managed to find a little sleep, he would often wake up confused, asking her where Daddy was. Now she spent her nights on the edge of sleep, just waiting for him to wake up, only to lose George all over again.

She flipped the sizzling eggs carefully. "I want you and your brother to try the schoolhouse today."

She was expecting a tempest flurry from her daughter and was therefore surprised when Annie said, "Okay, Momma."

Tabitha cracked a smile. "It'll be good for the both of you, I think. You haven't seen Orrin in a while, so maybe the two of you can go by Pete's store and get some hard candy."

Annie looked up from the plate. Her tired eyes, ringed with dark circles, brightened slightly. Tabitha thought she could have passed for five years older than thirteen.

"But last week when I asked about candy, you said—"

"That was last week." The words were harder than she'd intended. Why was it so hard to keep every conversation, even simple ones, from becoming an argument with Annie? It seemed all her daughter wanted to do was question every single thing she said. Annie had rarely been that way with her father, and the times she had questioned him, it usually ended with Annie laughing in his lap.

Even more infuriating was that Annie was right: they really didn't have the money. Tabitha would have to start selling things to try and make ends meet. George's pickax could be sold back to the general store for probably half of its cost. They would give her around five dollars for it. It wasn't much, but even if they gave her only a nickel, it would be worth it, if it gave her daughter something close to a smile again. Tabitha would have sold everything they owned just to make her children happy. The pickax would be the easiest to sell, as it was just a reminder of what she had lost.

She brought the skillet over to the table, put it down, and gingerly set the eggs onto the plates, their yolks like little yellow suns on a tin blue sky.

"I'll figure out the money," she said. "That's my job. You're working hard to go back to school, and that means you deserve a reward. People should get rewarded when they work hard." She'd hoped to see a smile on Annie's face.

Nothing.

She sighed.

"Okay, Momma," said Annie.

Their gazes met. It was a small agreement that passed between them, a first victory in what was going to be a long war with their grief.

Feeling her bottom lip start to tremble, Tabitha took the skillet and set it down on the stove. The iron clattered loudly as she looked out of the window.

Dunes of sand rolled out forever. Hundreds of miles of beach and not a drop of ocean. That is what her life had become, all grit and no salve.

But sadness wouldn't win today, she told herself. She had to find a way to stop crying in front of her children, even when it was hard. If they were going to work past their father's death, if they were ever going to find that strength in themselves, they had to see it in her first.

"I'm sorry, Momma," Annie said.

Tabitha's shoulders shook, her hands balled into tight fists. She took a deep breath. "I know it's hard to see anything happy since the funeral." She turned to look at her daughter with her eyes leaning on the wrinkled precipice of tears. "Let's start with this small happiness. Just a little sweetness that we can build on."

"Yes, ma'am."

Tabitha could feel the dam of emotion about to break, so she took her coffee cup, walked over to her daughter, and planted her lips in Annie's auburn hair.

She stayed there a long time, breathing in and out through her pursed lips.

"Wake your brother, get him dressed, then head off to school. I need to wash and go into town. Take some of the church bread for your lunch. I'll buy a chicken for tonight."

Back in her bedroom, alone, she clicked the door shut behind her and cupped her palm over her mouth to muffle her sobbing.

She bathed near the small table basin, trying to collect herself, then slipped into a dress and pulled her hair back into a tight bun. Sitting in front of the vanity, she didn't recognize the older woman looking back at her.

A knock came at the door.

"We're going, Momma," Annie said.

Tabitha opened the door, kissed both of her children, and gave two nickels to Annie with a wink.

She followed them outside. Standing on the porch, she watched them head down the main road.

Georgie turned around and waved to her, yelling loud as he could, "I love you, Momma!"

Tears in her eyes, she waved back.

He'd only taken a few steps before he turned and, waving again, hollered just as loud, "Annie loves you too!"

The Massacre at Yellow Hill

Tabitha, her empty, broken heart suddenly filled to its top, smiled. She kissed the tips of her fingers, filling her hand with all the love that might be carried in a mother's gesture and waved again.

Alone on the front porch she watched her children walk together, growing smaller against the bright vastness of all else. She considered them. Their circumstances. Wondering how she might make things last and dreaming of ways to change it all.

Chapter Three

YELLOW HILL, TEXAS

———————————

ANNIE AND GEORGIE walked beside each other along the powdery dirt road making up the main thoroughfare. They said nothing to each other. Walked in lockstep between the sand-blasted, peeling paint of the general stores, the Rusty Bucket saloon, Willie's Barbershop, the butcher and tailor shops. They took their time, happy to stay far behind the herd of children already filing up the road toward the whitewashed schoolhouse.

An ancient gargoyle draped in a blue dress and bonnet waited ominously in front of the schoolhouse, greeting the children in her usual deep voice. Schoolmarm Betty Williams, or the Marm as she was known among her pupils, had a clear purpose in life: she was destined to turn all sinister children into proper adults.

Boys and girls should be God-fearing, well mannered, and right handed. Students not meeting her standard would either be found on their tiptoes in a corner or sent home with welts on their wrists.

Annie, watching Marm Williams wave the children into the building with a long, thin rod clutched in her hand, rubbed her forearms. They had grown soft and tender during her time away from school,

Georgie kicked a rock. "Do we have to go today?"

"She's already seen us. So, unless you can sprout wings, yeah, we gotta go."

"Maybe if we walk real slow, she'll die before we get there."

"Momma wants us to go, so we're gonna go." Annie wrapped her arm around her brother's slender shoulders.

"All right, but if she swats me one time, I'm gonna kick her. Kick her so hard, she'll cry."

Annie pulled her brother to a stop and took him by the hand. "That'll only make it harder on Momma, Georgie. Plus, if you do that, you aren't going to get any candy later."

His eyes bloomed like a summer orchid. "Candy?"

Annie nodded. "Candy. After school. But only if you can keep yourself from acting up."

Georgie looked at Marm Williams, who was just a few yards away, her face wrinkled in a squint against the morning sun, something almost like a smile forming. "Come along, Millers," she called to them.

Georgie looked back at his sister, his face a mask of worry. He swallowed hard. "I'll do it for Momma…and a lemon drop the size of a silver dollar."

Annie laughed, and the unashamed sound startled her. She couldn't remember the last time it had floated out like that.

They were the last ones to march up to the door. Georgie broke away from Annie in a sprint, showing a bull-rider's bravery as he collided with Marm Williams's legs and wrapped his arms around her.

"Good morning!" The woman braced herself against the schoolhouse wall. The shock on her face made Annie wonder if this was Georgie's last-ditch effort to stop the Marm's heart with surprise.

The Massacre at Yellow Hill

Her mouth hung open. "Well, I, uh— Good morning, George Oliver Miller."

Georgie let go and strutted into the classroom as if he'd just won a great victory.

"Good morning," Annie said.

The Marm's normal grim countenance was softer than Annie remembered. Her pale green eyes showed with as much warmth as the woman seemed capable, which was only a little. "Good Morning, Annie Joy Miller. It's nice to have you and your brother back."

Annie bent a grin. "Thank you, ma'am."

"Plenty to catch up on," Marm Williams said, her face tightening. "But don't you worry. When the other children take their lunch, you and George Oliver can stay with me. You'll be caught up in no time."

Annie's shoulders sunk. "Yes, ma'am."

Lunch was when she'd hoped to talk to Orrin. He hadn't come by the house since the funeral. She guessed that his parents hadn't thought it proper for a visit until the Millers extended an invitation. His parents were like that.

As she walked into the schoolhouse, she looked to Orrin's desk. Her friend, skinny as a rail with ears as big as a jackrabbit's, had his face planted in a book. She shoved through two girls giggling in the aisle and made her way to the seat next to his.

"Excuse me, young man," she said, trying to sound like the schoolmarm, "but those adventure books are not part of a proper education." She slapped him on the shoulder.

Jostled from his story, Orrin said, "Hey—" His look of annoyance melted into a big buck-toothed smile. "Annie!"

She smiled back at him, "Hey, Slim, got time to get some candy after the old lady gets done boring us to death?"

His smirk drooped. "Gah, Pa wants me to sweep the stable after school, but we can stop in at his store just before then."

"Count on it."

His smile returned, higher and toothier than before. "Perfect."

Annie opened her desk and found her chalk and board right where she'd left them. The dusty white letters still read, 'I wish I was anywhere else.'

She and Orrin had been writing each other notes on the boards during arithmetic only a month ago. A statement about boredom now sent her into a spiral. Those faded words had been written when her father was still alive, and now, though the letters remained, they took on a much different meaning.

"All right, children, everyone sit and settle," Marm Williams said as she took her place in front of the chalkboard at the front of the room.

When the room remained buzzing with chatter, she whipped the desk hard with her switch. The sharp crack silenced the room, straightening every spine, every shoulder shooting erect to its full height.

"Hey," Orrin said, daring a hard whisper, "I'm really glad you're back." He always knew just what to say.

"Me too," Annie lied. She wished she could be anywhere else, so long as it was back when she'd written on the small board inside her desk. A time when her father was still warm and real.

She realized that today would be the first time in her life she would walk up to the house after school and her father wouldn't be standing in the doorway, smoking a pipe with a smile, ready to ask about her day.

Chapter Four

YELLOW HILL, TEXAS

A SILVER BELL ABOVE the general store's door jingled, announcing Tabitha's arrival. Pete Adolphus, his white smock draped over a brown twill shirt, was standing behind the counter sliding tins of tobacco into a glass-faced cabinet.

He turned. The faint surprise that passed over his face quickly lifted into a cordial smile. "Mrs. Miller, good morning."

Tabitha walked up to the counter and hoisted the pickax. She misjudged the weight, and it fell heavier than she'd wanted. Flecks of iron and dust loosed from the grip and head, peppering the white countertop.

She barreled forward with her words. "I need to see what you'll give me for this." She'd never really bartered before, but she had watched George trade many times, and so she knew her best bet was to be curt.

"Well, we don't normally—"

Tabitha gave a cautionary, exasperated sigh.

Pete stopped, his mind putting the pieces together swiftly. "Well, I suppose I could take a look."

He pretended to give the tool a thorough examination through his spectacles, a hum escaping his throat. "Well, it has some chipping here, and the rust doesn't help, but I'd say—"

The doorbell jingled again. Tabitha turned to see Charlie Gathers and Lucas Ramos walking in. The foreman froze, cringing like a scolded dog. Lucas Ramos, a heavyset Mexican, bumped into the back of him.

"What the hell, Charlie," Lucas said.

Charlie took off his hat. "Morning, ma'am."

Tabitha nodded politely then turned back to the shopkeeper. "What's it going to be, Pete?"

"We sell these for four dollars, ma'am. I can offer a dollar and a half to buy it back."

Tabitha's heart fell into her stomach.

Charlie and Lucas walked up beside them, looking at the tobacco tins Pete had just put up, both of them doing a piss-poor job of pretending like they weren't listening to the widow's conversation.

"Four dollars," Tabitha said. "I don't see much wrong with this pickax. Any man could swing it and get his job done just as well as if he owned one of those new ones."

Pete's face wrinkled, insulted. Then he looked at the foreman, and slowly his lips peeled back, smiling foxlike, revealing his crooked teeth.

"Charlie," he said, "you know about picks more than just about anyone I can imagine. What with you running the mine and all. Tell me, what would you give for this one here?"

Dim as a candle burned to the wick, the foreman looked at the pickax and scoffed. "That thing's busted near to the edge of its iron and the haft is warped. Hell, I wouldn't give fifty cents—"

"George took excellent care of his tools, Mr. Gathers." Tabitha was fuming. She could feel fresh heat boiling on her forehead.

The Massacre at Yellow Hill

"Seeing as they were the thing that kept a roof over our heads and bread on our table."

She looked back over at Pete, who was smiling as he nodded at Charlie. It was over. There was no chance she'd get her asking price, not now. These men were dumb as stumps and didn't have a lick of kindness in their hearts.

"You heard him, Mrs. Miller," Pete said. "I couldn't give more than a dollar knowing the opinion of such an expert."

Lucas spoke up. "That George's pick, huh?"

"What's it to you?" Tabitha snapped at him. Her eyes stabbed back over to Pete. "A dollar. You cut fifty cents off the offer just to save yourself half a bill? How many times have we fed Orrin at our table, Pete? How many times have you and Judy enjoyed our hospitality?"

In a fever, she grabbed the pickax by the haft, jerking it into her hands like a weapon.

"And you, Charlie Gathers, you come to my house in the middle of the night, tell me that my husband is gone from this world with only an 'I'm sorry, but these things happen?' My husband was twice the man of any of you are. Honest, fair, and he would never have refused any of you anything he could have given."

Before she knew what was happening, the pick was high in the air. She swung down hard, smashing the flat blade into a crate of tomatoes, hewing through the wood.

"Christ almighty," Charlie said, jumping back.

Pete hollered, "Aw, shit. Not my tomatoes, Tabitha! This ain't the goddamn mine!"

Tabitha spun. "Don't you dare say my name." She tried to compose herself, but the heat of her anger swelled in her chest, threatening to burst out of her with the kind of violence she'd never dreamed she was capable. "I'll show you what this damn thing can do. A dollar! I'll show you what George's pick is really worth."

She raised the pick again, thinking she'd cleave a wound right into the countertop.

But then a thought passed over her mind, slicing right through the anger and the grief. An idea—thanks to Peter Adolphus.

Tabitha lowered the pick, setting its heavy head on the ground. She curled loose strands of blonde hair away from her eyes around her ear and turned to the foreman. "Charlie," she said, "I'd like to see Mr. Hart immediately."

"You mean, like, right now?" His face was a mask of confusion.

She squared her eyes on him like a hawk and took a firm grip of the tool. "Right. Now."

It was Lucas Ramos who, eyeing her warily, said, "You best do like she says."

Tabitha Miller got more than her share of queer looks as she pounded along the dusty main street of town with Charlie Gathers hobbling behind her. The head of the pick hung over her shoulder, glinting red in the late morning light like a giant's rusty razor. She ignored the stares from the blacksmith, the baker. And, at the gawking of the coach manager Willie Jones inside the livery stable, she barked, "Piss on your look, Willie."

Willie, shocked by her rebuke, shivered so hard that his black stovepipe top hat tipped back to reveal his bald head.

Charlie Gathers tried to match Tabitha's stride, but with his injured leg, he struggled to keep up with her. "Hey. Hey, slow down. You can't just— I said slow down, goddamn it."

Tabitha did not slow. Small beads of sweat formed on her head, wetting her yellow hair for lack of a bonnet. She didn't care. She was pushing headlong into demand. Not into a proposition or a request

The Massacre at Yellow Hill

but a straight-fucking-forward expectation. Ever since George had brought them to Texas, they had tried to trade, always getting the raw end of the deal. They had tried to buy their way into subsistence, but the land had swallowed their money as quickly as it drank the water. The world had taken enough. More specifically, Jeremiah Hart had taken more than he was owed, and had shown no charity or kindness upon George's death. The mine had taken her husband's nights, and then, his life. As a married couple they had asked and asked of the world, toiled in its earth, and come up short.

Tabitha Miller was done asking.

She strode up to the bottom of a hillock just at the edge of town, where she approached the gaudy home of Jeramiah Hart. Blue as a sapphire in the morning light, the freshly painted, two-story jewel was perched atop a swath of grass kept green by a fancy pump-irrigation system. Hart owned his own aquifer, of course, solely apportioned to ensure that his yard overflowed with grace and wild clover.

A young man in a white shirt and black trousers stood at the water pump in the front yard, cranking the lever up and down. Water sloshed into a bucket at his feet, splashing the tops of his boots.

"Excuse me," said Tabitha.

The man looked up and spied Tabitha approaching. He stopped working the handle, took out a silk handkerchief, and wiped his brow.

Micah Hart, Jeremiah Hart's son and only child, was dark-haired, with moonlight skin completely resistant to the withering sun. He watched, wringing the handkerchief between his hands. "Mornin' ma'am," he said. "Something I can help you with?"

Tabitha's dress, damp around the armpits and hips, swished around her body as she stomped into the yard, still angry as a bull.

"Where is your pa?"

Charlie came dragging his bum leg up behind her. "Mrs. Miller, I said you can't just barge up here like this." He reached over and grabbed her by the meat of her bicep. "Listen now——"

The widow's eyes flashed in her rage. She swung the pickax in a flat arc, leveled directly at Charlie's head.

Charlie, eyes widening in horror, threw his hands up in defense, but Micah reached out and the wooden shaft slapped into his grip. "Whoa, whoa. Easy," he said.

Tabitha's head began to clear, but she was still fuming with anger when she jerked hard on the handle, trying to wrench the pickax from his hand.

"I'm here to see your pa, Micah. You go tell him that I won't be put off. It's the least he owes me for what happened to my husband." She sighed, wiping the sweat from her forehead. "For what is happening to my family."

There was a deep calm about the boy, a cunning in his eyes much older than his years. "I'll go tell my father you're here, but only if you promise not to take another swing at Mr. Gathers here. And Charlie," Micah said, his eyes flattening hard on the foreman, "don't put your hands on Mrs. Miller again."

Much to her surprise, the older foreman didn't buck the youth.

"Yes, sir," was all Charlie said.

Tabitha followed Micah up to the porch, where he asked her to wait.

She did so, all the while glaring out into the ocean of sand in the far distance, not speaking nor looking at Charlie. She'd had enough of him today and forever.

After a few minutes, Micah came back and invited Tabitha into the house.

Entering, she looked around the home. This was her first time inside, seeing as she and George were not the kind of people who the

The Massacre at Yellow Hill

Harts would call on to join them for supper. She marveled at the vast finery of the interior. The rugs were thick and plush, most of them a variation on a yellow floral pattern traced with scarlet and brown. A long carpet, matching the rugs in color, ran up the middle of the stairs. Next to it, a sloping banister served as a handrail. Its custom trim and polish caught the sunlight, leaning so straight and true that whoever had made it would have been insulted to be called just a carpenter.

The stairwell curved, bending out of sight to the right of a crystal chandelier on a long silver chain. The chandelier caught a thousand sunbursts in every facet of its tear-shaped stones.

"Oh…," escaped Tabitha's lips.

The awe she was feeling—that heart-flutter pause of surprise when something beautiful suddenly steps out from behind the curtain of the mundane world—was spoiled entirely when her gaze caught the custom china cabinets sheltering a dinner set more valuable than everything she owned. Next to the cabinets was a masterfully worked buffet table draped in linen. Atop the spotless linen, an enameled hand basin gleamed as if it had never once been used. Outrage overtook her awe.

How could a man have so much and share so little of it with the people who made all his wealth possible? Her grip tightened on the pickax.

Micah gestured for her to follow him, and they climbed the stairs together. The runner beneath her was so plush she could feel the softness through her boots. For a moment, just a moment and no longer, she imagined what it would be like to live in a house like this. And then, for a longer time, she imagined how satisfying it would be to burn the damn place down.

They hooked around the curve of the stairs and stopped on the landing. There were four rooms set two-by-two, their furnishings hidden behind heavy doors, all spruce except one. That one was strange. Black as iron. Through its center ran a heavy bolt that extended the entire width of the door, then disappeared into the wall.

"Father's study is this way. You can leave that here, ma'am." He gestured at the tool still leaning on her shoulder.

Tabitha clutched the pickax tighter. "I'll worry about the pickax. You just lead the way."

A little brass handle hung from a chain attached to a fitting in the ceiling.

Micah took the handle and pulled it. Somewhere, bells jingled.

"Enter," came a muffled voice behind the door.

When the young man put both hands on the door and began to pull, Tabitha saw the effort it took to open it. The door wasn't black as iron, she thought; the door *was* iron.

As they stepped into the room, Tabitha looked at the frame of the door, which was also iron. She guessed that the whole wall had been reinforced with it.

Hart was sitting behind a large desk that was big and square, red as a candied apple. Wearing thin spectacles, he looked up from where he was scribbling along slender columns in a large book that Tabitha suspected was his money ledger. As much as he liked to boast that he could buy the town ten times over, he was probably reading over his books to remind himself of that very fact.

The bowl-shaped study had rounded walls stuffed with hundreds of books, all of them looking old though not mistreated. It smelled of old leather and tobacco smoke, and a musky aroma she could not place. Brightly lit, the room was shot through with sunlight beaming in blue shafts from a large colored glass dome. Light mingled with glass painted the study in a dusk blue hue.

"Mrs. Miller," Hart said, his voice sharp as the nib of the fountain pen perched in his hand. "My condolences, firstly, for your loss.

The Massacre at Yellow Hill

Secondly, my apologies that I was unable to attend the wake or the burial. As you can see"—he gestured with a flourish of his wrist, the cap of his fountain pen rolling in a tiny circle—"I am a man with many obligations." A touch of annoyance was in his courtesy.

He gave a hard look at the pickax resting on her shoulder, then pointed the pen at it. "I hope you aren't planning to club me with that like you tried to do to my foreman."

There was a heaviness to his words, something that made Tabitha's knees want to shake, but her grief had been heavier, and the thought of her children begging in the street steeled her spine.

"Mr. Gathers told me that if our son was old enough to swing a pick, you'd give him a job at the same price you were paying my late husband," she said.

Hart nodded slowly. "That is mostly true. I said I'd hire him at half your husband's wages, him being new to the work and all."

"Well, my boy is ten and isn't ready for that kind of labor."

"I agree," he said. "The boy should finish his schooling, lest he get in the way of real men doing hard labor in a hard place. Every child should be allowed their softness until the world demands for them to callus over."

Tabitha lifted the pick off her shoulder, letting the head clap down on the floor.

Hart's eyebrows furrowed.

"Give me the job."

Hart leaned back in the chair, eyes widening. He licked his lips and smiled the shape of hidden anger, as if insulted. He looked at Micah, then back to the widow. "Come again?"

"You heard me."

"Mrs. Miller," he began, the words an exasperated sigh. "I am certain that your grief has pushed you to the very limit of your mental navigation, but you must consider me either insane or stupid if you think I'm going to allow a woman to bust stones for me. The impropriety of it alone—"

"I'm not asking, Jeremiah," Tabitha said. "I'm telling."

His eyebrows jumped to his hairline, eyes flaring. "I'm sorry?"

"I'm telling you that when my children go to school tomorrow, I will be walking down the road from them in the opposite direction. Down the same road that my husband walked to make sure that our livelihood was secure. I'm going to be there, busting stones and carving out rock, in the place where my husband lost his life. And do you know what you're going to do, Jeremiah?"

The rich man shifted, sucked his teeth.

"You're going to pay me to do it at a dollar more an hour than you paid my husband."

"And why would I do that?" His voice was cold and flat. Seething quietly.

"Because you took the most important person in my world from me. And you didn't just take his last breath, you took him from us every night. Every night. You paid him practically nothing, and still he gave you everything. You owe for what was lost to us, and I think a dollar more on top of practically nothing is worth the peace that justice provides. I believe it will make a brightening of your greedy soul, Mr. Hart."

She could hear his teeth grinding together in aggravation, see the cold smoking embers in his eyes trying to wilt her countenance, but the rightness of her demand was the shield which protected her from Hart's wilting stare.

"Your husband was a hard worker. And I do hope you'll pardon me when I tell you plainly that I believe your grief has robbed you of your fucking senses—"

The Massacre at Yellow Hill

"How many men did you lose? How many workers are laid up because of the fire that broke out?" she said, not asking. "You need labor, and it's not like folks are streaming into this town every day. Don't let the dress fool you, Mr. Hart; my hands can chew through stone just as good as any man. Hell, I've already got the tools."

Hart cocked his head. His eyes flicked to Micah, standing behind her, then back to her. "Well, aren't you clever. You're right. We are desperately behind schedule. A half dollar more than what George made, and Charlie has his right to cut you loose the moment you can't keep up. And if that deal doesn't strike you as fair, well then it's time to get the hell out of my house. And thank you for your visit."

"You are the worst kind of man," she said. "For you, too much will never be enough. You see strength only in yourself and weakness everywhere else. I'm a mother, and that's a strength you'll never know. And my hands will callous quick as any man's.

Hart was furious. "You may think you want to hew rock now, while your hands are still soft and your back is straight as an arrow, Mrs. Miller. But know that this job isn't a courtesy or charity. You want to work for me? Fine. But the ultimate eventuality of time and gender will be on you. And when it happens, don't you dare come to this house looking for pity. Don't you darken this doorstep with that pick ever again, or I'll consider it a premeditated act to do harm on my family, you crazy bitch."

"Pa!" Micah snapped. "Control yourself."

"Quiet, boy," said Jeremiah, leaning his eyes hard on his son.

Tabitha just shook her head. "I've always known you were a bastard, Jeremiah. I'm glad that others are getting to see it, too."

Hart blasted out of his chair, his hands slamming on his desk. "Get out!"

Tabitha swung the pick over her shoulder, turned, and looked at Micah.

"I'll see myself out." And she did, smiling her first honest smile since she'd lost George.

Chapter Five

YELLOW HILL, TX

THREE MILES FROM the Hart estate, Mark Marple stepped into the mouth of the mine. His hands, slippery with sweat, gripped the shaft of his pick and held his oil lamp ahead of him. The grimy light revealed the progress they'd made since the cave-in on the main shaft. Fresh timbers were braced against the wall and flickering lanterns hung from hooks, ready to be freshly wicked, filled with oil, and set alight.

The flame from his lamp did not carry far and the tunnel was very dark. He took a deep breath and looked behind him at Larry, the canary perched on a twig inside a wire-mesh cage. The bird, yellow as the sun, whistled his bright song.

"You let me know if you smell anything, okay, Larry?"

The bird twisted its head from left to right, tweeting. Mark didn't know why, but the sound of birdsong had always made him feel good. Larry wasn't his first bird, of course. Mark had had many birds before, and it was important to select just the right name, he thought. You couldn't name a bird just anything; there had to be a kind of poetry about it. The first had been Barry Canary, then his brother, who'd come from the same clutch, Terry Canary, then Carrie Canary, and of course, poor Jerry Canary, who had been with them the night George Miller died.

The last few weeks, though, Larry's song had been no exception to that rule. Right up until the night-shift miners had busted through the rock wall that had formed during the cave-in.

Only he, Charlie, and Lucas had seen what had gotten hold of George Miller in the dark. He'd even had the sense to pop a few rounds off from his revolver, though he wasn't sure if they'd hit their target. However, the whole shaft had broken in on itself over the creature, so he'd told himself it had been killed either way. What still unsettled him, though, was that when the miners had finished hauling out the stones from the cave-in, they found no corpse of the creature. Some of the caliche had dark stains splashed on it, but he didn't know if it was George's blood or the thing that had opened George from shoulder to groin. The sight of that rending would never leave his mind.

Mark told himself that most likely, the wolf—or whatever it had been—had retreated into the deeper branches of the mine and found a dark place to lay down and die. Animals did that all the time. At least, that's what he'd heard.

Besides, it was half a month ago now, and the thing needed food, didn't it? He didn't know of any creature that could live half a month without eating. So, he was reasonably sure that no animal could possibly survive under those conditions, but what the hell did the son of a blacksmith know about the capacity of animals? The only animal Mark needed a clear reckoning on was good old Larry Canary, singing his melody.

He stood at the neck of the main shaft, watching the yellow light lick the walls then vanish into complete blackness.

The Massacre at Yellow Hill

He put down his pickax and touched the outside of his right pocket, feeling the edges of the tinderbox. He pawed at his other pocket where the outline of his little derringer revolver jutted against his pants. He switched the lamp to his left hand, just to be sure that if he had to jerk his revolver out fast, he could.

Taking a deep breath, he reminded himself that someone trustworthy and important had to be the lamplighter. You couldn't trust just anyone with making sure the lamps were properly positioned sixteen feet apart. Refueling at the right time was also a skill. It took a particular kind of genius, he thought, to do this job. An innate sense of timing things right, knowing when the men would quit for lunch so that neither his work nor the lamps running out of oil didn't impede their progress.

And good Lord, what if a man without steady hands were given this task?

Fire.

The lamp oil would splash all over the ground and you could have another pocket explosion.

Mark Marple, emboldened by his understanding of how important his job was, bent down, picked up the canary cage, and walked into the pitch black, whistling along with Larry.

Chapter Six

YELLOW HILL, TX

THE APPLE BREAD had been the only redeeming aspect of lunch, and even that had been stale. Annie still munched on it while scrawling cursive letters on the big chalkboard.

Georgie sat at his desk. He sighed, buried his nose deep in his reader. She knew that sigh, knew the quality of misery bound up in its sound.

Lunch ended for the other children, and in one ruckus of sweat and laughter, they came in and sat at their desks.

Orrin was panting as he sat down next to Annie. "Whew. You missed a great game of tag."

Annie rolled her eyes over to him. "Don't rub it in," she said, then crammed the rest of the bread into her mouth, stuffing it full.

Orrin laughed.

The rest of the day had been grammar and numbers, neither of which Annie cared much for. She liked reading more than other subjects, but every distraction from what was waiting for her and Georgie after school, and after the general store, was a welcome one.

When Marm Williams dismissed class, Georgie was the first to stand. He rushed out of the front door with his arms raised high in the air like he had won a race.

Though Marm Williams called after him, Georgie paid her no mind. Captivity was over; now came the fresh freedom of the afternoon. Orrin and Annie, along with the other children, gathered their things and laughed as they watched the boy tearing down the road back toward town.

"Where do you think he's headed?" asked Orrin, letting Annie step out the door first.

"I don't know where he's going, but I know where he's about to be."

"Huh?"

"Just give him a second. He's about to remember that Momma gave me our nickels to spend on candy."

Annie might have been a fortune teller gazing into a crystal ball, because at that moment Georgie skidded to a dead stop. He turned, looking back as Orrin and Annie began walking down the road toward the center of town.

It took Georgie twice as long to run back, and, when he reached them, he was all out of breath with sweat dripping down his face.

"I—" He took in huge gulps of air. "I for—"

"Catch your breath, Georgie," said Annie.

The boy, hands on his knees and chest working like a bellows, smiled as he shook his head.

They let him catch his breath, then started again back along the main road, which cut through a short mesquite thicket.

"I'm sorry I haven't been by since, ya know, your pa—" Orrin began. "The funeral, I mean." His hands were in his pockets, eyes tracing his steps. "My parents said that your ma would let them know when it was all right to visit. When I didn't hear anything from y'all, I got worried. Like we were done being friends."

"Done being friends? Do people stop being friends just because they don't see each other for a long piece of time?" she asked, not liking that notion one bit.

Orrin shrugged. "I dunno. I just know I don't want it to happen to us.

Annie bumped her shoulder roughly into Orrin. "Not a chance, Slim."

"Ow." Orrin rubbed his shoulder.

"Things have just been hard since—" She couldn't bring herself to say more. "You know?"

"My mother said to tell your ma that if y'all want to come to supper, they'd like that. All of y'all are invited. Mother just needs to know when so she can be prepared."

"That's nice. I'll let Momma know." One of the things Annie had noticed after her father's passing was that when people thought you were sad, they all wanted to give you food. There had been food at the wake, food after the wake, and pies and breads and cookies that people had brought over from something called a love offering, which made Annie think that if you loved someone, you gave them a bunch of sweets.

Accompanied by a whole gaggle of ladies in bonnets, most of whom Annie had never met, the saloon owner and Deacon of the Methodist church Lyle Collins came to the house after the funeral with gaunt Reverend Callum. After all the ladies in bonnets had dropped off their sweet breads and pastries, Annie had seen Mr. Collins give her mother an envelope. When her mother looked inside, she hugged Mr. Collins very roughly and started crying again.

"So just tell me what day your ma thinks is best," Orrin said, "and I'll tell Mother, and y'all can come over. It'll be fun. I can show you my new rifle."

Annie's eyes went wide. "Can I try it?"

"Sure, long as Father says so. We can shoot cans off the fence, if it isn't too late. He won't let me shoot after the sun goes down. He says that causes tomfoolery."

"Tomfoolery?" Georgie said, picking up a rock and chucking it into the tangle of mesquites. "What's that?"

"I'm actually not sure. Father says it all the time when he starts talking about the miners and roughnecks that go to the saloon late at night. Says they are up to tomfoolery," Orrin said, nodding as if agreeing with himself. "Sounds like a real problem."

Schoolhouse, mesquites, and the falling sun now behind them, they stepped off the main street and into the general store. Orrin's father was standing on a stepladder, reaching for a tin of tea.

Below him, giving orders, was a large woman in a blue dress. Her red hair stuck out like wire beneath her bonnet. "Not the Irish tea, Pete. I said I want the Earl Grey."

Mr. Adolphus grunted and reached higher, balancing on one leg on the ladder. "Yes, ma'am." He looked back over his shoulder and saw the children. "Afternoon, Millers. Son."

Annie and Georgie responded in unison, "Hello."

"Hello, Father," Orrin said.

They knew the rules in the general store. Mr. Adolphus was happy to let children without an adult make purchases, unless they hazarded to touch anything they weren't going to buy. There was also no yelling in the store. And no running. He made these rules abundantly clear to every single Sally and Joe who jingled the silver bell above his door. Those who broke any of these rules were exiled, never to gaze upon lollipop or candy cane ever again.

The Massacre at Yellow Hill

"I see that school is out. I'm guessing you must be here for…?" Pete let the question hang in the air.

Georgie blurted out, "Candy!"

"Give me just a"—his fingertips finally reached the tin of tea—"just a second. Be looking for what you want."

The children turned and looked at the back wall behind the countertop. It was a sight that never failed to turn a child's eyes the size of dinner plates and set their mouths dripping like starving foxes. A dozen crystal clear glass jars, their lids twisting upward like bishops on a chess board, stood in a long row. Gumdrops, licorice, jawbreakers, sugar sticks, and, of course, standing perfectly in the middle of it all, were Georgie's yellow lemon drops.

"This is why adults get jobs," said Georgie. "This is why people have money."

"Georgie, my friend," Orrin said, "I couldn't agree more."

Annie reached into the pocket her mother had sewn into her dress and rubbed the two nickels together.

"I think I'm going to try something new today," Georgie said.

Annie rolled her eyes. "You say that every time."

"No, I don't."

"Sure do," she said. "You're gonna look at all of them for a long time, and then when Mr. Adolphus tells you to hurry, you're going to get the lemon drops, and you're always glad you did."

"No question for me," Orrin said.

"Candy canes?" asked Annie.

"All other choices are folly."

Annie looked at the jawbreakers and the gumdrops, which were her normal favorites, but something about the salt-water taffy sounded interesting. She'd never tasted salt-water or taffy, but at five cents for two pieces, such a high cost, it must be the best candy ever made.

Georgie could keep his sticky lemon drops and Orrin his candy canes; Annie was going to be bold with her nickel today.

After Mr. Adolphus helped the woman with the tea, he came over and opened the jar of candy canes. Orrin's gray eyes gawked among the spiraling red and white shepherd's hooks, a smile stretching across his face.

"Speak none of this to your mother," said Mr. Adolphus, his own smile foreshadowing what Orrin's would one day become.

Georgie was true to form, waffling about while asking if he could smell the contents of each and every jar. In the end, Mr. Adolphus dropped five lemon drops into his hand.

When the shopkeeper looked at Annie, she said, "Salt-water taffy, please."

He narrowed his eyes at her playfully and leaned on the countertop. "That's just two pieces for a nickel, sweetheart. Are you sure?"

Annie didn't hesitate. She plucked the two nickels from her pocket and said, "Never more sure in my life."

He opened the jar in front of her and tipped the aperture toward her. "Red is my favorite, but blue and pink are both very good."

Annie plucked the pieces wrapped in thin waxy paper. She smiled. She'd picked a blue one, her favorite color, and green, because it reminded her of the color of her father's eyes.

The children stepped out into the hot afternoon. While Orrin and Georgie quickly put their candy into their mouths, Annie slowly unwrapped the paper around the blue taffy.

The boys looked at her, mystified in wonder to see what would happen when she ate it.

The taffy was thick, so sticky that it almost glued her teeth together as she chomped in big loud smacks. "Itsss good," she said, all the saliva in her mouth making a hiss of the words. Her eyes rolled in delight and she smiled.

Both the boys sighed, relieved.

"What about the green one?" Georgie eyed her.

"I'll eat it later," Annie said, having absolutely no intention to ever do such a thing.

Chapter Seven

YELLOW HILL, TX

WHEN HE LIT the last lamp, Mark was careful to slide the glass fixture over the flame so that it did not go out. He looked back the way he'd come. The places where the light did not touch seemed to shift and bend as if alive.

Larry Canary whistled his happy song, still twisting his tiny head left and right with each new measure. The high notes ricocheted around the bend of the tunnel, turning the bird's solo into a choir of yellow birds in that dark place.

Mark felt a cool wind brush his sweat-soaked neck, as if someone had just blown on the nape of his spine. A shrill cry burst out of his lips, and he fumbled in his pocket for his revolver, hoping not to blow his pecker off. He spun to face what he envisioned to be the giant, sharp-fanged creature that had mauled George Miller.

There was nothing.

Just a wall of jagged stone the miners would begin working on again when the next shift came stumbling back to work, ragged and bleary eyed.

Heart hammering in his chest and sweat dripping off the curled edges of his stringy hair into his eyes, Mark wiped the sweat away with a quivering hand.

Larry the Canary peeped. Starting his song again.

Mark jumped at the sound. Then, had to laugh.

Shaking his head, thinking himself silly, he was about to slide his gun back into the holster when he heard a whistle.

Not the tweeting of any canary, but a low hooting sound. He picked up his lamp with a trembling hand, the light swirling into the shadowy places before him.

whoooooooooo

The sound was soft, like the questioning of an owl. Low like the voice of the devil, he thought. He stepped toward the wall. The sound died out for a moment, then picked back up again.

whooooooooooo whoooo

Mark squinted and stretched the lamp toward the wall, where he spied a hole in the stone. It was small and jagged with a rush of air spilling through.

whooooooooo

It was probably the entrance to a pocket in the rock. Some place that allowed the wind to rush in through an aperture and weave around the hidden hollow.

When he got close enough for the air to rush against his face, the smell hit him square in the nose, hard as a punch. Fetid and stale, reminding him of his time among the slave quarters on a Mississippi plantation some twenty years gone. It was the smell of shit and disease and decay.

whoooooooo

A fresh blast hit him in the mouth. He gagged, the thick odor threatening to upend his stomach. Whatever was behind this stony wall had been there a long time. Maybe it was some kind of mass grave full of Native Indians killed by rangers during the territorial disputes. Mark didn't know, and he didn't care to guess further.

whooooo click-click

A sound like falling stones. No, the sound had moisture to it. If it was an aquifer, he would have been able to hear droplets falling from limestone or shale formations.

Curiosity overtaking cowardice, Mark tucked the derringer back into his pocket. He tugged his leather glove off and gingerly slipped his pointer finger inside the opening. It reached far enough inside the rock to just curl around the formation on the other side. The surface felt warm and wet, a slick sheen coating the stone. It didn't feel like stone at all.

More curious now than afraid, he slid his finger into the little hole. He gave a tug but the rock stayed fast, too thick to be pulled away.

Something wet slithered around his finger. He screamed and tried suddenly to pull away. There was a slash of pain, and a loud wet pop.

Holding his quivering hand up to the light, he looked for his index finger among the shadows. Where his finger should have been, there was only a stump flooding over with fresh hot blood.

With his other hand, he shoved the revolver barrel into the hole. Pulling the hammer back, he howled in pain, firing all six rounds into the black abyss. The sharp tang of gunpowder stung his nostrils. The repeat was deafening.

The echoes died away.

All went quiet.

No whistling.

No birdsong.

He cursed the hole and tried to jerk his revolver free, but it didn't move. He pulled again, only to realized that the gun wasn't jammed; rather, something was holding onto the barrel and pulling on it. The unseen force gave a hard jerk, grinding the gun-barrel further into the hole.

Terrified, he let go of the grip and watched as the cylinder began to slam against the wall. The steel smashed into the stone over and over like a pumping quartz crusher, trying to pull the weapon through the wall.

The gun sparked as it burst through the other side, breaking open a space in the rock as wide as a man's waist.

Though there was not much light, Mark saw some tremendous white, vein-streaked flesh pulsing among the flickering shadows. A dark line running the entire width of the visible skin broke open, revealing a terrible mouth. Inside were many rows of needled teeth.

Dozens of snake-like tongues whipped about inside the maw, one loosely curled around his ruined revolver. Another, twisting around in a tiny loop, clutched the pink flesh of his finger.

The mouth, alive with hunger, opened even wider, the flopping tongues whipping themselves turgid.

He turned to run, but his back was punctured through with what felt like railroad spikes hammered by a steam-powered driver. He felt the tongues twisting, violating his flesh. He opened his mouth to scream, but no sound escaped his lips. The tongues slithered around his spine and curled around his guts. The last thing Mark Marple ever felt was a tendril coiling around his beating heart before it jerked it free of his chest.

The last thing he ever saw was Larry Canary's face.

The bird was fluttering wildly in his wire-mesh cage, screaming a song Mark had never heard before.

Chapter Eight

YELLOW HILL, TX

TABITHA WAS SITTING in George's rocking chair, slipping the needle into a pair of work trousers when Annie and Georgie came through the front door.

"Hey, you two," she said, her eyes narrowing on the cuff of the pants. "How was your first day back?"

"It was fine," Georgie said. He walked over to the rocker and hugged her tightly around the neck. Only ten years old, but already he carried an unfettered strength about him, always squeezing hard as he could. A boy with an unvarnished heart, his love was insistent, immediate, irrepressible. Love of the rarest type, found only in the innocent and unashamed. "We worked numbers while everyone else got to have their lunch outside," he said. "But, Mom, Mom!" A sudden enthusiasm expanding in his voice. "Look!" He reached into his pocket and produced three little candies, yellow and sticky and sweet.

Tabitha looked into his emerald eyes, where she found a shimmer of George in their hue. "Three left. I'm so proud. Now, promise you'll save those until tomorrow. Dinner's soon."

Tabitha looked up at Annie. She was still standing just inside the doorway, a puzzled look on her face.

"What's wrong, sweetheart?"

Annie's face twisted. "What are you doing to Daddy's pants?"

"Well," Tabitha said, setting the sewing in her lap, "I need to talk to the two of you about that very thing. See, I went into town today to try and sell your father's tool to Mr. Adolphus."

"You what?"

"Just listen, sweetheart. I didn't end up selling it. Besides, that penny-pincher—"

"You're selling Pa's clothes." Annie's eyes flared.

Tabitha shook her head. "No, no. Anyhow, Mr. Adolphus isn't the point. The point is, I got a job today, and it's not going to be easy but…I've got your father's job."

"You— You're going to work in the mine?"

"I spoke to Mr. Hart about it today. Well, I say I spoke, I really let him—" She stopped speaking when she saw Annie's eyes widen not with excitement but with horror. Slowly, her daughter began to shake her head and took a step back.

"You can't," said Annie.

Tabitha's mouth went slack.

A long string of tension jerked taut in the room.

Georgie looked at Annie, then back to Tabitha. "That's where the rocks killed Daddy. What if that happens to you?"

Tabitha reached out and stroked her son's face. "That's not going to happen."

Georgie pulled back from her, as if afraid. "You don't know that."

"You can't," Annie said again.

"Y'all don't understand. We don't have enough money to—"

"I don't care. I don't care if it means all of Mr. Hart's money and the whole town. You can't do this."

The Massacre at Yellow Hill

"I don't want you to get hurt. Please don't go, Momma." Georgie's bottom lip began to tremble.

Tabitha shook her head again. "I have to do this." She tried to tell them how she went to the Hart House, how she stood up to the man who had sucked the marrow out of her husband's strength. Tabitha had stood up to the most powerful man in the entire town, undertaking a task George had never had the courage to do himself.

"If you do this, I will never forgive you." Annie's tone cut deeply.

Georgie started to sob. "I don't want you to get hurt, Momma."

Tabitha tried to explain to Georgie, tried to put her hands at his soft cheeks but the little boy turned away from her. She tried to tell him everything would be okay, that she could make everything all right for them again.

"If daddy can die," said Georgie, his big green eyes welling with tears, "that means you can die. My heart hurts so much already from missing him. Please don't make me miss you too."

Tabitha threw her arms around her son. She held him close, so close that no matter where the boy's heart broke her arms would be there to catch every piece. That was her job. No matter how deeply his grief would cut her, she would catch every shard. She could not piece that heart back together. No one could, only time. But she could open herself and protect the boy from shattering in a lonely place.

Annie stepped closer, nearing the embrace. For a moment, Tabitha thought her daughter would join their hug. But the tears in her eyes were not born from sorrow. Annie was not sad. She was furious.

"Daddy would never let you—"

"Your father is gone!" Everything she had done today—her strength and personal triumph in standing up to Hart, her good work coming home to prepare for tomorrow at the mine—all of it spoiled. "Your father is gone, and we have nothing, Annie. No money, no food. If I don't do this, we— we aren't going to make it."

Georgie squeezed her shoulders with all the strength in his small arms. "Do something else, Momma, anything else. Please."

She pulled away gently, though her voice remained stern. "There is nothing else, George Oliver. This is it. In this town, there are ranch hands, miners, a single schoolteacher, and the whores at the saloon. Is that what you want? Do you want your mother to spend her nights, while her children are sleeping—"

"No," he said, though she knew he didn't totally understand. "I just want you to be safe."

Annie just stood there, shaking her head indignantly.

All of Tabitha's rage, the fury she had met Hart with, resurfaced. She aimed it at Annie. "I am your mother, and I will provide for this family. Your father is gone, and I'm alone."

"Stop saying that!" Annie stamped her feet.

"He's gone, Annie, and I miss him more than the two of you could ever know."

It had come out of her mouth without consideration for its effect. Annie's mouth broke open into a sob as she ran toward her room.

Tabitha looked at Georgie. "Wait, I didn't mean—"

Georgie lowered his head. "I want Daddy."

She wanted to wrap her son in her arms, but some strange shame held her in place. She dropped the sewing onto the floor, along with the half-finished trousers. "I know," she said. "I want him too, honey."

Georgie, revealing once again his brave and unashamed love, wrapped his arms around her legs with all his little, crushing strength. Pressing his hot face into her skirts, he cried out with a sound that broke Tabitha's heart all over again. It was in that moment she truly understood that nothing would ever be the same again.

Chapter Nine

YELLOW HILL, TX

LUCAS RAMOS CAME galloping up to the house on a horse that had been shot out of a cannon. The mare, hot in a fresh lather, skidded to a stop as he pulled the reins tight and low. He didn't so much dismount as fall off the horse and then hurriedly knotted the leather straps to the hitching post.

He pounded on the front door, leaving a smear of red on the white paint.

When no one came immediately, he twisted the knob and found it unlocked.

"Mr. Hart," he bellowed. Then, forgetting all measure of proper behavior, he pushed inside and bounded up the stairs to the iron door. He reached for the chain but stopped when he saw a thin crescent of light slashing between the wall and the door.

"Mr. Hart, sir," he called again.

When he heard no reply, he placed his hand on the door and pulled it open.

The sight snatched the wind right out of his lungs. Jeremiah Hart was sitting at his desk, his palms flat on the desk, his mouth slack and his eyes rolled up into his head. His lips were moving, whispering words that Lucas could not understand.

"M-Mister Hart." The words came out of his mouth as more of a reaction than deliberate thought.

On the desk was an open book, its pages strange, made not of paper but of something like tanned animal hide.

Leaning over to look, Lucas saw strange symbols and words scribbled in jagged penmanship.

Hart sat there, the whites of his eyes like pearls floating in raw, bloody milk.

Reaching out with trembling fingers, Lucas touched one of Hart's wrists. "B-b-boss?"

Wherever Hart's mind had been, it came thundering back into his body. When his consciousness hit his active mind, he gave a loud, furious scream, first a hard exhalation then a primal noise as loud as a train whistle.

The sound startled Lucas so badly he screamed too. Hart's pupils, wide as dimes, zeroed in on Lucas. There was a burning fire in those eyes, something higher and more dangerous than anger.

"What the fuck are you doing in my house, Ramos?"

"The mine, boss. We need you at the mine."

Hart shook his head violently, trying to clear whatever had been rolling around inside his skull. "Goddamn it. Where is Gathers?"

Lucas gave his employer a grim look. "He's the one sent me up to the house, Mr. Hart. Said the last time someone got killed, he didn't think to talk to you first."

His full faculties began to return. "Cave-in?"

Lucas gravely shook his head.

"Ride back. Pull everyone out of the mine. I'll be right behind you."

"Yes, sir." Lucas turned to leave.

The Massacre at Yellow Hill

"Wait," Hart said, stopping him. "Two things: One, tell all of the men on site to go home and get their guns. If people ask, tell them we are hunting a pack of coyotes that took up near the mine."

Lucas nodded.

"Second, and I cannot stress this to you enough, Ramos, whatever you saw or think you saw, forget it."

Lucas nodded. "Y-yes, sir."

"Now get. Tell Gathers what I said."

Lucas backed out of the room slowly. "Yes, boss."

Lucas pounded down the stairs, gripping the curled railing hard as his flailing feet dared to skelter out from underneath him.

Like a blast furnace, the setting sun hit him hard when he came out of the shade of the porch. His horse was wet with sweat and still breathing hard, but he straddled the mare anyway, kicked her, and made a thundering push for the mine. The slack-jawed face of Hart, the lolling tongue twisting inside his whispering mouth, was stamped into his mind's eye.

He wondered if he had enough money stashed away to leave Yellow Hill. All he had to do was get to the mine, tell Gathers what Hart said, give the mare a feed, and then he could get out of this place before it claimed another life.

But where would he go? Big Spring was the nearest town, but it was sixty miles of hard riding with very little water and supplies, and there were the roaming wolf packs to consider, and dozens of miles of road choked with mesquite bushes sheltering rattlesnakes, scorpions, and black-widow spiders. And those natural predators were a small fear compared to the human danger awaiting on the trail. There were road bandits. Gangs roaming the edges of the road, waiting for the brave, the unaware, and travelers so desperate they would risk to travel alone.

All these perils stacked themselves on one side of his choice.

On the other side was the face of Jeremiah Hart and the thing that had ripped George Miller open like an old wine skin.

And, riding hard toward the mine, the scales tipped one way in the mind of Lucas Ramos.

He'd leave Yellow Hill that very night.

Micah jostled in his saddle as he and his father came upon the mining camp just after dusk. There were two dozen men already there, those who did not own a revolver were armed with shotguns and rifles. Most of them had absconded with the guns they now carried after the South called it quits in the War. Jeremiah had taken no part in that conflict, but he'd hired men who had fought with the Confederacy, because it seemed to him that there was a deep camaraderie there, one bound up in both a cultural idealism and a fraternal idiocy. He'd confessed to Micah that he'd found a way to bend both of those to his advantage. He hired no Black workers, not because he despised them but because he didn't want to bother with the headache of them working with those who'd fought for slaver's rights to own them. That was smart thinking by Micah's reasoning.

As soon as they clopped up to the buzzing mass of men, all huddled around a large fire at the base of camp, he saw the fear in their eyes.

"Where the hell is Gathers?" his father barked at them, in clear command.

Lucas stepped out of the huddle. Micah noticed a caution in his eyes. "He's in the main tent, boss."

Jeremiah turned to Micah and nodded in the direction of the tent.

The Massacre at Yellow Hill

They dismounted, and Micah followed his father through the collection of miners. Jeremiah pounded a path to the tent and ripped back the canvas flap. The smell of ripe death hit him in the face. Micah wanted to retch, but when his father gave no inclination of letting the rank odor bother him, he swallowed the thick saliva in his throat and stepped around to look at what lay inside.

The boots were stained black from dried blood, the legs perforated with holes clear through the calves and thighs. There was nothing left above the hips but a thick tangle of purple and red and black.

Charlie Gathers, with one knee anchored in the dirt next to what was left of the body, glared at Jeremiah. "Weren't no wolf or damn bear that did this, boss."

His father slashed a look at the foreman. "Reckon you're right, Mr. Gathers." The tone was a cold, hard thing.

"Something is in the mine, Mr. Hart. Whatever it was ripped Mark here in two. Tore him up like this. Some of the boys said they seen it, boss."

"What the hell was he doing in there alone?"

"Relighting the lamps. Did you hear me say they seen it?"

"Of course I did. Well, what the hell was it?"

Charlie hollered, "Josh, come on in here!"

A man just a few years older than Micah pushed through the flap.

"Sit," his father said, pointing to the ground next to Charlie.

The boy, hat in his hands and eyes as wide as a frightened doe, did as he was told.

"Speak, boy," said Jeremiah. Tell it all."

The young miner's voice came out quavering. "We was all taking a meal at camp when we heard Mark's revolver come banging out of the shaft, so we all dropped our plates and came a running. But it's a good ways, so it took a minute or two. I was the first one in and…"

There was no sympathy in his father's voice: "And what?"

The boy looked down, closing his eyes to keep from having to look at what was left of the lamplighter.

"Ah, Jesus Christ, Mr. Hart. Uh." The boy's mouth trembled. "It had a hold of him, half-swallowed inside its mouth. Like a snake that's just nabbed a rat. I couldn't be sure of what I was seeing at first. Me and the first group of fellas kicked up a lot of dirt when we came to a stop. But when the dust settled, we saw it."

"Goddamn you, boy, just tell me what it was that had him."

The frightened miner looked over at Charlie as if unsure of what to say, his mouth frozen open.

"Don't look at him," his father snapped. "Look at me."

"I don't know, Mr. Hart."

"Don't know?"

Charlie stood up. "Other men said the same thing as Josh here, said it was wide as a bear and white as an opossum, but with skin nothing like either. Round body with a big mouth. Derry was at the front, said he got the best look...saying it looked like a worm that was as big as a man. And when they approached, the thing snapped Mark in half and slithered back into a new shaft they hadn't seen before."

"How many of the men have seen this body?"

"W-we pulled Mark out," Josh stammered, "and someone else got his bird. Ah God, that thing was going crazy, half-beat itself to death trying to get out of the cage."

"How many?"

Confused, Josh stammered again. "E-everybody, sir. They all seen it."

"Micah," his father said, " take Josh outside and tell those boys to gather round the fire while I talk to the foreman." Jeremiah's gaze fell upon Charlie, his nostrils flaring.

The Massacre at Yellow Hill

Micah pulled the flap back and gestured to Josh. "Come on, son," he said, though the miner was his senior.

"You keep your mouth shut till I tell you otherwise," his father said.

Micah was unsure if he was talking to both of them.

The fire was a good piece away from the tent, but his father's angry bellowing at Charlie carried easily to the men standing around it. Then, surprisingly, the voice of Charlie Gathers boomed back.

Micah watched the miners around the fire, their faces in absolute disbelief at what they were hearing. People in Yellow Hill didn't yell at Jeremiah Hart; that would be like playing a game of chance against the Grim Reaper. You might win, but who would dare to try in the first place.

Though many of them tried to hide it, the miners glanced at him uneasily, as if unsure of how to address him. He'd been out at the mine many times, but he'd never been among them without his father. When he caught their eye, he gave them a hard nod of his head, a gesture of mutual respect he'd seen his father use on many occasions. A few of the men nodded back, others just looked away. One, a grimy old man with rotting teeth and half an ear missing, looked Micah right in the eye and then hocked a giant wad of tobacco on the ground.

Micah steeled his spine and lifted his shoulders to full height. "Problem, old-timer?"

The miner narrowed his eyes. "Don't be looking over this way with those glares, young blood." Though diminished by time, the old man was heavy with corded muscle, still broad and not yet bent at the shoulders.

All eyes fell on Micah, and the shuffling of their boots as they moved away kicked up a swirl of dust between him and the old miner, as a lane opened between the two men. The fire crackled as if the charred mesquite within the flames sparked with anticipation.

"I figure I'll look where I please. I wasn't trying to ruffle your feathers. No harm done, I figure." Micah hadn't worked in the mine his whole life, but he wasn't the prim dandy these workers surely suspected he was. His father had him working with horses and rope and hay bales and carpentry since his sixth birthday, and he was a skilled boxer too. He wasn't about to take guff from someone who would one day be hoping Micah signed off on his wages.

"Reckon I say you don't look this way again, lest you want to shit out those pretty teeth tomorrow morning." The old miner smiled with menace.

A thin, ragged man put his arm across the old man's chest, trying to calm him, "Take it easy, Marty."

A left hand snapped out like a rattlesnake and took the thin man right on the chin. His knees slapped together and he dropped face-first into the dirt.

The crowd let out a holler.

"All of you shut yer damn mouths," said Marty. "Ain't no man gonna put his hands on me"—he pointed a finger at Micah—"or look on me in such a fashion."

From the crowd, someone shouted, "Damn it, Marty, look what you done to Earl!"

Earl rolled over, moaning on the ground.

"You're makin' a mistake tussling with Hart's son," a man said, hidden among the rest.

"Kiss my ass, Tanner," Marty said. "I don't give a good goddamn whose snatch this kid fell out of. I ain't getting cowed by him, nor nobody else here. Hell, the Harts are the reason that my friend, and a good man, is dead. Fuck all that. Two men!" He lifted two fingers up for the crowd. "Don't forget what happened to George."

"I don't know what happened to those two men," Micah said, "but it isn't my family's fault those men are dead!" He stepped closer to Marty, ready to defend his family's honor.

"The fuck it ain't. Yer daddy sent George into that mine, and he sent Mark Marple in there after him. Both of them torn apart for what? Two dollars a day. Charlie told us he let that asshole know what happened, about what kind of thing we found in that fucking hole, but Hart made Charlie lie about it. Forced him and Mark and Lucas there bust George up with hammers to make it look like he'd gotten smashed in the cave-in. He's making us all lie about it. Lie to our families. And if we don't, well by God, he'll fire us. The rest of the hands are too chickenshit to say it, but we all know he'll do worse if we speak out. Well, I'm too old to give a shit any longer, and I ain't too old to whip a little spoiled shit like you for looking at me that way."

Micah shook his head. "Fuck you."

The old man's eyes widened, and he took a step toward Micah. "Well, by god—"

Ramos pushed through the crowd of men and stepped between the angry miner and Micah, who was ready to kick up dirt over Marty's accusations.

"He's telling the truth, boy," Lucas said. "Mr. Hart made us bust up George's body, and he knew that there was some kind of predator in that mine. He knew all along."

Micah turned back to the tent. Inside, their voices still raged. Shaking his head in disbelief, he turned back to the motley crew of men. He looked at their dusty clothes all thick with dark powder and he scanned their eyes.

There was no deceit among them. They were cowards, Micah thought. All of them willing to blame his father for what had happened, but weren't they responsible for their own safety?

Why hadn't they armed themselves and taken action after the first attack?

"All right, old-timer," Micah said as he pushed his palm heavily down on the butt of his revolver. "You wanna blame these deaths on me and mine, well, let's see what you think when one of us does what you cowards couldn't."

"Easy, boy," Lucas said, his palm upturned at Micah. In the other was a rifle.

"Ain't no easy about it! You all want to bitch and moan about the mine being unsafe—well, I say we go in there and make it safe. Hell, you all got rifles and revolvers. How about we go in there and take matters into our own hands?"

Micah expected the men to rally to him, but that didn't happen. They all just stared at him, lazy stupidity or cowardice on each of their faces.

"You go in that mine," Lucas said, "you ain't coming out alive."

Micah smirked. "That's a no from the nutless Mexican. How about the rest of you? What about you, old-timer? You got a pair of peaches between those legs, or have your balls shriveled to raisins? You want to go into that mine with me and skin the thing that killed your friend?"

"Hold on, Micah," Lucas Ramos said. "We oughta wait for your pa. He wouldn't want you going into that mine alone. All these men—" He swung his arm behind him, gesturing at all the miners who had come close to the mine entrance to see what was going to happen with Micah and Marty, but no closer than was absolutely necessary. "If you'll wait, your pa is gonna order them all to go in there with their guns and knives, and they'll go. Only an idiot would go into that cave alone, Micah."

Jeremiah Hart had taught his son a singular guiding principle, a way of thinking that, he said, separated generals and soldiers, wheat from chaff: Above all else, you must never fear to take action. Do what others are unwilling to do. When he becomes a man, a Hart never follows men; men follow a Hart.

That truth was immutable. Harts never doubted themselves and they never feared the repercussions of decisive action.

"Doubt, Mr. Ramos, makes cowards of you all," Micah said. "We're going into that mine and I'm going to come out again after I've killed whatever predator those men were too weak to face."

Marty grunted. "Boy's for it, Ramos. And, hell, I figure if we get into a tussle, we can shoot our way out of the mine, and you boys can ambush the thing if it makes chase of us. Y'all get set up over there."

"Come on, old-timer," said Micah, smiling. "Let's go kill this son of a bitch." He turned and started toward the entrance, his revolver dangling heavily at his thigh.

Marty looked at Lucas, shrugged, and then followed after young Hart, shotgun slanted over his shoulder.

"No," said Lucas.

Micah and Marty turned to look back.

The Mexican stood there, painted in all the color of the wavering firelight, his head cocked to one side, shaking slowly. He gazed upon the miner and the youth with a relaxed purpose in his eyes.

The eyes of a man who has all at once made a decision. Or perhaps, the sight of a decision that all at once has made the man.

"Lucas?" asked Micah, more an insistence than inquiry.

Lucas Ramos stood there looking at those two men looking at him. He took a deep breath. Then turned and walked toward his horse.

"Lucas, get back here," Micah commanded.

But the Mexican did not answer, walking until the firelight drained from his form and the shadows spilled over him completely.

"Lucas!" Micah now demanded. "Get back here."

Outside of the firelight came the sounds of a horse riding away. It was only while the sound of the horse's hooves chopping of the hard caliche diminished, that Micah saw rider and horse rise to the top of a dune. Their silhouettes were, for a moment ensconced in starlight, riding across the horizon, before they sank out of sight.

"Goddamn Mexican," said Micah.

Marty laughed. "Goddamn yourself, kid. The quickest, best shot out of this entire outfit just left. We could have used him."

"Damn him," he said. "Now come on. I'm worth ten of that son of a bitch with a gun."

Micah walked inside the foul-smelling shaft, Marty at his side. An odor, rank as maggoty meat, hit them on a strange wind originating from deep inside the mine. Lamps lined the walls sending shadows whipping and curling like dancing black devils against the stone.

Marty swung his shotgun off his shoulder and placed it against the young man's chest, stopping him. "Hold it," he said. "Listen to that."

Micah tilted his ear toward the long chamber. A gentle whistle swung through his hearing, then receded, and came again. As the sound quieted, he felt a soft breeze carrying the smell of a long-resting tomb broken open down a shaft that despite the lamps was very long and very dark.

"There must be a place where the wind is entering," Micah said.

Marty peered into the twisting lamplight. "And what about the smell?"

The Massacre at Yellow Hill

Micah pushed the man's shotgun away from his chest. "Probably carrion from the beast's kills, brought back here through the opening on the other side. It likely hunts at night and has made its nest in some kind of antechamber."

Marty looked at Micah with a crooked glance. "Boy, you can say all them words—hell, you can even believe them—but it's clear you don't have shit for sense. At least not for mining. There ain't no other opening. Above us is all sand and sand and sand for a hundred miles. This ain't no natural cave. We didn't find this shaft; we dug it out over time looking for that green vein of stone your father wanted to find so badly. See here." He reached over to run a finger along a pale vein streaking through the rock like St. Elmo's Fire.

"What are you suggesting then?

"Ain't suggesting, I'm telling. Breeze coming down this shaft ain't coming from an opening above."

"Well…" Micah broke open his revolver and checked the rounds even though he knew they were there and ready. "We aren't going to kill this thing standing around here."

Marty gave the young man a broken-toothed smile the color of buttermilk. "You got grit, boy. I'll give ya that. More than your daddy does, at least. Lead on."

The deeper into the mine they went, the hotter and more rank the wind became. Sweat dripped down Micah's face in tiny streams, the sudden humidity so thick his shirt clung to his chest. Pulse racing, he felt the ticking of his heartbeat against the revolver grip. He swallowed hard and blinked heavily.

The oil lamps flickered shadowy limbs along the long bone-white shale walls. Pressing further in, they came to a dark bloodstain pooled upon the ground. Along one of the streaks of blood, they found a twisted corpse of metal: the cylinder and barrel of a little revolver. Thin gashes ran along the housing. Micah searched nearby, but the revolver's grip was nowhere to be found.

Ahead of them, the wall had broken open to reveal a cave or chamber of some kind. Inside the hole, wide enough for two men to stand abreast, was a darkness black as oil.

The power of the odor coming from the chamber turned Micah's guts over. A bit of his lunch came up in his throat, but he swallowed it back down so as to not embarrass himself in front of the old miner.

"Ah, God, that is rank. Kind of rot I ain't never smelled," the old miner said. He flapped a grimy rag out of his back pocket and slapped it against his nose and mouth.

"Grab a lamp." Micah jerked on one of the wall lamps. It came loose with a grinding noise and a puff of caliche dust.

They stepped over the rubble from the fallen wall, into the chamber. The light from their lamps pressed against the darkness. Micah expected the light to touch the walls of the chamber, but the cave must be too large.

The rank wind hit him in the chest, hotter still. He looked over to see Marty's lamp guttering in the dark. The miner's face was illuminated, revealing terror in his wide eyes.

"Go back and get another lamp," Micah said. "We'll need more light."

"We already got two, and I'll be damned if I'm gonna be caught holding two lamps and not my scattergun with that predator about."

"Stay here then." Micah retraced their steps and exited the chamber back into the shaft. He holstered his gun and wrenched another oil lamp out of the wall.

When he made it back, he found Marty had stepped back into the main shaft, standing next to the aperture.

The Massacre at Yellow Hill

"What are you doing back out here? I told you to stay in there," said Micah.

The old miner shrugged, defensive. "Well, I sure as hell wasn't going to stand in there alone like an idiot."

Micah gave him no mind as he stepped back into the darkness. He set down one lamp and snuffed out the other.

"That was fucking pointless." The older man was growing impatient with him.

Holding the end of the doused lamp, Micah slung his arm out in a short arc. A slapping wet sound hit the ground. Over and over again, he swung the lamp a little harder each time. When it was empty, he took the lamp that was still lit and touched its flame along the ground.

With a sudden woosh, the oil ignited a river of flame all along the floor of the cave. The twisting light illuminated a fiery path that reached far enough to touch the edges of the chamber.

The cave wall sloped up reaching, taller than he had expected. Walls of twinkling emerald light shone wet in the flickering fire along the ground.

Stepping along the river of flame, Micah walked to the edge where the ground sloped into darkness. There was a sound. A strangeness to it.

From behind him, Marty let out a yelping cry that was quickly muffled.

Micah turned and pulled his revolver. "What is it?" he cried out.

Then his eyes went wide.

He screamed.

Part II

PTOLEMY & SON

Chapter Ten

BIG SPRING, TX

MARTHA PRIMMON'S EYES nearly bulged out of her head when she saw the Black man in the brown duster riding through the evening dark into Big Spring with a little white boy on the saddle behind him. They rode a weathered yellow mare. Mouth agape, Martha hiked her skirts to her ankles and shuffled down into the muddy street.

She was a reserved woman, God-fearing, and proper. Her mother had taught her that opinions were best kept as silent observations, unless the situation merited a woman's keen intervention. Wisdom was a quiet force, she knew, but when she saw the boy in the company of a Black man, it was her obligation to say...say something.

Sloshing through the muck, Martha thrust her hands out in front of the horse. The big man at the reins brought the horse to a halt.

"Excuse me, but, young man, where on earth are your parents?" She gave the man no mind, peering around him.

The boy was thin of feature with hawkish green eyes, his face the color of cold moonlight that ended in a sharp point for a chin.

The early etching of a hard life on the road had already wrinkled his young brow. He leaned in the saddle to look at the woman, then he looked to the man holding the reins.

The Black man's voice was a heavy thing, his words clipped short by his large pronounced teeth. "Answer the lady."

The boy turned back to the woman. "They're dead, ma'am."

Martha Primmon slapped a hand against her chest, inhaling so swiftly the air seemed to inflate her eyes. "How awful. And you were forced to take passage with this…man. Dreadful. Just dreadful."

"Out of the way," the man said.

Martha stood her ground, her arms springing away from her body as if she'd just been crucified. "No. And how dare you say such a thing to me, you…" But she stopped herself short.

The man stared at her, his eyes languid. Bored. "This horse is about to move, lady. I don't reckon you'll want to be standing there when she does."

"Are you *threatening* me?" Martha's face burned hot as a stoked fire. Sweat trickled down her eyebrows. This kind of exertion for her was rarer than Christmas Eve, but someone had to stand up to this uncouth retch. "Why, I'll go get Sheriff Smoot and he'll show you!" She peered around him again to speak to the boy. "Son, you come off that horse and we'll get you some place safe."

The boy's face was wrinkled in confusion. "Ma'am, Mr. Ptolemy here, he means what he says. I think you should move."

He didn't know. Poor mercy, the boy had been with this supposed Ptolemy too long to remember the rules of society. No clue that he was like the prodigal son, eating pearls with swine while far away from civilization.

Martha Primmon narrowed her eyes at the man. "Sheriff Smoot will have plenty to say about this."

The Massacre at Yellow Hill

Ptolemy sighed, then gave the horse a squeeze.

Martha, a sentinel in the street, gave a huff as they rode around her, and when they were out of earshot she whispered to herself. "We sure will," she said. "We'll see right quick."

She hurried out of the street and stomped down the walkway to the sheriff's office.

On the mare, hands wrapped around Gilbert Ptolemy's waist, Carson looked about the town, watching people stop along the street. Though none of them halted the horse's progress as the fat woman had, they all looked at Mr. Ptolemy with shocked faces. It was all too familiar.

"Folks are so strange," the boy said.

"How you figure?" Ptolemy asked, guiding the horse down the street.

"They act like this before we help them, but they act differently after."

"For a time, sure. Then when they don't need you, you go back to just being someone that ain't like them. We just ain't stayed in a place long enough for you to see them switch back to that simple way of thinking." Ptolemy rode up to a large square building that squatted near the center of town. Above the many lamplit hitching posts swung a sign that read, 'The Black Mustang Saloon.'

"Tie us up," Ptolemy said.

The boy swung his leg over and slid belly first off the horse's hind end, his boots plopping into the mud.

"Now, no matter what, when we get inside, you stick to what we talked about."

The boy took the reins. "Yes, sir." He tied the straps around the hitch in a simple knot that would pull free quickly from one end but wouldn't budge if the mare got spooked.

"Eyes and ears open. Mind clear," Ptolemy said as he reached into a pouch strapped over the horn of the saddle. He pulled out a ripe green apple. He dismounted while keeping an eye on the winged doors of the saloon, caressing the horse's neck as he offered her the apple.

"Vanilla likes those apples, don't she?" Carson said with a smile as he watched the horse's big lips pull back and chomp into the fruit.

"All beautiful women love sweets," Ptolemy said, rubbing the bridge of Vanilla's long nose. "You be good now."

They climbed the boardwalk to the wing doors. Wild laughter billowed outside the saloon over the top of someone banging away on a piano, a singsong tune unfamiliar to Ptolemy. Carson parted the doors and Ptolemy followed him in. Having Carson go before him always seemed to soften the blow of seeing a Black man come in the front door of a place filled with white folks. People would figure he was a bodyguard or servant who accompanied the thirteen-year-old white boy on his father's errands. Part of that was true enough; Ptolemy did watch over the boy, but he was his own man.

Inside, dancing upon an elevated stage, a women bundled in a scarlet corset and matching silk skirts danced. She twirled above her audience and then kicked high at each piercing piano key bang. With each flourish of her legs she flashed an incomparable smile along with her white bloomers. A bramble of drunken cowpokes sat at circular tables just below the stage, hooting and hollering, begging the dancer for kisses and proclaiming their adoration. She sent their hearts tumbling down lust's staircase with only a smile, a wink, and another kick.

The Massacre at Yellow Hill

Ptolemy followed Carson past the piano next to a leaning staircase and over to the walnut bar to the left of the stage. Behind the bar's shining bass fixtures, one of the largest mirrors he'd ever seen reflected the saloon behind him and multiplied the dozens of bottles on the shelf into hundreds. In the middle of the mirror, a dark horse reared under swirling etched letters that read "The Black Mustang." A short, pigeon-faced man stood behind the bar, stacking glittering whiskey glasses into shining towers.

Ptolemy turned, looking up to the second story where he saw closed doors, likely for pleasure and for let.

"Well, what in the hell is this," came from the bar.

Ptolemy shot his gaze over to the high-pitched voice of the bartender, whose droopy eyes were narrowed at Ptolemy and the boy.

The dancer saw them next, the sight stole her dance along with her pearly smile. When she stopped dancing, the men at the tables turned around to see, and the piano choked on a minor chord and died.

"Boy, you can't bring him in here." The bartender circled around the bar. In his hands he clutched a club. The knob at the end was dark wood, about the size of the apple Vanilla had eaten.

Ptolemy didn't move. Carson took a step toward the barkeep, his voice high and sweet, "My name is Billy Waterson, sir, and this here is my father's man, Warren. And, sir, please let your mercy shine through here. He is charged to stay at my side at all times. Daddy told me that folks in this town would respect the wishes of a gentleman and that I shouldn't fear to come here, on his behalf, to barter for cattle."

The bartender dared to look away from Ptolemy to address the boy, the club clutched tightly in his hands. "Who's your daddy, boy?"

"Judge Hezekiah Ellison, sir. Our beef comes by way of Abilene. On land newly possessed on account of the tragedy currently beset on our old holdings in Georgia. Daddy said folks would understand our loss if I mentioned General Sherman, though he said I am too young to fully understand his full meaning by the name."

Wringing the club handle in his hands, the bartender's face sloped to a frown. "I know your meaning, young man, and I am sorry to hear of difficulties for your family. But there ain't no way *that*"—he pointed at Ptolemy—"is gonna sit in here and drink our beer or our whiskey. 'Specially not toting an iron on his hip."

Carson frowned. "So then you'll agree that if my father's man relinquishes his revolver, we can sit and wait for our potential buyer?"

"Who you waitin' on?"

"Mortimer Gail of Sweetwater, sir. My father made it awful clear that a place like the Black Mustang would be the perfect meeting joint for Mortimer and his six sons, whom I'm given to barter with. I'm even supposed to pay for all their 'wants,' as Daddy put it. Though I'm afraid the one hundred and eighty dollars he entrusted to me with might just barely cover the costs."

The bartender's droopy eyes suddenly bloomed open and a smile crossed his lips. "Hell, why didn't you say his name sooner, son. I am well aware of Mr. Gail and his holdings." Then he looked up at the tables of cowboys listening in on the conversation. He barked at the piano player, "Get your ass back on them keys, Mike, and get Shirley dancing!"

The musician's shoulders jumped at the command, and his fingers sprang to life again with a new tune.

Shirley tossed her skirts high, giving all onlookers a flash of her silky whites.

Placing his hand on the boy's shoulder, the bartender pulled him closer as he lowered his voice. "I'm willing to let your father's man reside in here, so long as he surrenders his firearm to me. For safe keeping, you understand." He gave Ptolemy a hard stare up and down. "And that big knife of his. You keep him to himself, and I think the Mustang will be happy to be the place of safe financial transaction between civilized people."

Carson said, "The Ellisons thank you, Mister…?"

"Grouper. Jonas Grouper, my boy. Owner, founder, and proprietor."

"Of course, Mr. Grouper. We'll keep to ourselves until our other party arrives. And I'll start with a glass of beer, please." Carson turned back and looked at Ptolemy with a false air of command. "Warren, your sidearm and skinning knife, please."

Ptolemy gave the gun and the knife to Grouper, the small man's hands shaking when the Walker Colt hit his fingers.

"Mister Billy," Ptolemy said, "might I have a beer too? I worked up a powerful thirst on our trip."

Carson shook his head, a look of pained frustration on his face. "Warren, how can you be so selfish as to wear out our host's hospitality? And take off your hat. Manners!"

Ptolemy feigned a grimace and obeyed.

Carson looked back at Grouper with doe-wide eyes. "I apologize."

Grouper nodded his head. "I know. I know, son, some folks just ain't ever gonna get it. I'll have your beer brought over to your table. Please have a seat."

They sat down at a table at the rear of the saloon where they could see Vanilla outside and the whole span of the main street. From time to time, one of the half-drunk cattlemen would turn to look back at them but would quickly return to Shirley's flailing skirts.

"I hate doing this," Carson said.

"You did well," Ptolemy said. "Now we can get to work."

"I don't like talking like that to you."

"It's about why you say something, son, not always what you say."

Carson's countenance wilted. "I just wish there was another way."

"Sometimes there is," said Ptolemy. "Just not in places like this."

A homely girl around Carson's age sauntered over to the table and handed him a mug of beer. She batted her eyes at him. But he kept his eyes away from hers as he shooed her away with a thank you.

Ptolemy smiled. "She seems nice."

"Yeah, so?" said Carson. The boy scanned the saloon, his eyes low. "The woman on stage, right?" he asked.

"You're getting a seasoned eye for this," said Ptolemy. He kept his chin tucked into his throat, making sure no one spied the two of them speaking as equals in the open. "More importantly than being right, tell me how you know you're right."

"The way she moves: it's like other women and it ain't like other women. Like she's pretending to try hard, when she don't have to try at all."

"Not bad, but what's the dead giveaway?"

"I figure she's been dancin' all night, and she ain't got a drop of sweat on her."

Ptolemy stifled a smile. "Good. Now, how do we kill it?"

"Like we did in Monroeville, I guess. Silver buckshot, then removal of the head."

"Just like in Monroeville, huh?"

Carson sipped his beer, his face flushing from booze and confidence. "Sure, why not?"

"You given any thought to the thralls she's got going on over there?"

"Thralls?"

"Didn't have those to deal with in Alabama, did we? A thrall is a slave to the creature's will. Once she notices what's goin' on, she'll sic them on us faster than hounds. And seeing as my gun and knife are behind that bar over there, I guess you're reckoning to gun them all down with your sawed-off."

"I didn't—"

"Sip your beer. Relax. Remember, you're a cattleman's boy here with his servant, waiting on seven randy cowboys, all with a powerful thirst that'll put lots of dollars in the pocket of that greedy piss pot behind the bar."

"We could come back in the morning. She'd be sleeping then, and the men would be gone."

"That might work, sure, if we knew where the thing's resting spot was. But who's to say she doesn't have Grouper protecting her by day? Are you ready to kill a man who is likely under the influence of a creature such as her, likely compelled to act such as he does? Now, I'd love to hang him for thinking that I'm any less a creature of God than they are, but we don't hang folks just because they got hate in their hearts."

"So, what do we do?" asked Carson.

"First, we relax," he said, then looked around the bar, his dark brown eyes catching those of a cowboy who kept turning around to glower at him. "Well, Shirley over there has all these cowpokes by the balls. There's only one thing that men feel more powerfully than lust, son—hate. We're gonna save these dickheads' lives with just that."

The cowboy who had glowered at them turned to look back at Shirley, insatiably drawn to her.

"We only have one chance at this. And I got news for you, if it don't go perfect"—he smiled at the boy—"we're probably gonna end up dead"

"That's not exactly an encouraging word."

"You just do like I say," Ptolemy said, as he rose from the table. "Most importantly, when she does what she's gonna do, you rely on those hands of yours. Steady. Sure."

Carson nodded. "Yes, sir."

"Now, if you'll excuse me," Ptolemy said, "I've got to go save a bunch of White folks by picking a fight with them."

Ptolemy got up and walked toward Grouper. The pigeon-faced man was filling a mug with beer. Ptolemy leaned against the brass lip of the bar then set his hat down on the bar. "Believe I'll have me one of those beers, barkeep."

Grouper looked up with a smile that quickly melted. "That so? Well, I think you'll be having you a beating far worse than anything you got from that boy's daddy if you don't go sit your black ass back down."

"The thing I never understood about you folks," Ptolemy said, "was how y'all could be so angry at a people that ain't got nothing while you all live like kings in your desires."

Grouper reached behind the bar. Ptolemy's legs tensed, thinking the bartender was going for a revolver. But when his hand came up with the big club in his hand, Ptolemy relaxed again.

"That's 'cause you've got a malformed brain, boy."

"I'm born from Adam, same as you," said Ptolemy.

"The hell you are. You don't understand the natural order of things—no creature hatched from some egg in the jungle can ken the way God has ordered His world. So let me make it real clear." Grouper rapped the thick head of the club on the bar. "Adam was created, pink as a babe. Folks like you sullied the world when God scattered the white race to the wind for tryin' to build a tower to Heaven. You're a people created as a punishment for men thinking they could reach the eternal kingdom. Just like you're gonna get punished for coming over here for forgetting the natural hierarchy."

"I see," Ptolemy said coolly, then snatched Grouper by the hair and smashed his face into the walnut bar.

The Massacre at Yellow Hill

The dull, wet crunch of the man's nose breaking wasn't quite loud enough to resound over the piano playing. No one had even looked away from Shirley's swiveling hips, so he walked around the bar, retrieved his revolver out from under the counter, and slipped it into his holster. Then he took his knife into his hand.

Grouper was out cold on the floor, splayed open at the legs. A veil of blood masked the bartender's face, and the bridge of his nose was bent now, crooked as a river. His eyes rolled up into his head when Ptolemy took him by the hair and wrenched him to his feet. He placed the razor-sharp edge of the skinning knife to Grouper's throat. With just a little pressure, blood welled along the blade.

Ptolemy cleared his throat, then hollered over the piano music. "Gentlemen, I believe that Mr. Grouper has had a change of heart regarding the policy of who can be served at the Black Mustang."

All the men previously caught in the glow of Shirley's erotic dance looked back at the bar. At first, they were confused, then their white faces became pink, slowly working their way to mad-as-hell red.

Ptolemy smiled. "A miracle-on-the-way-to-Damascus kinda thing. Though it appears painful now, I am sure one day soon, he will, like the Apostle Paul, realize the full sorrow of his folly."

"What in the hell?" A cowhand, bigger than even Ptolemy, stood up so fast his belly caught the lip of the table, flipping it over. Beer and whiskey glasses crashed to the floor.

Another man pointed over at the bar. "That son-of-a-whore's got Jonas."

They came in a rush at first. All of them drawing their revolvers and knives.

The table flipper said, "You're a dead man."

Using the groggy Grouper as a shield, Ptolemy dug the blade of his knife a little deeper into his neck to draw a few more pearls of blood. "All I wanted was a goddamn beer."

Grouper, now back among the conscious, fully understood his situation. He cried out, "Somebody kill this mother—"

Ptolemy reached between the bar owner's legs and grabbed him by the balls. He gave the mass a threatening squeeze. "Another incitement like that and I will permanently unman you." He slanted a gaze to his captive. "Maybe that's why you're so damn angry. Hell, I'd be mad too if my nuts was small as yours."

Over the jostling mob, Ptolemy watched Carson slip behind the crowd and approach beautiful, dangerous Shirley. The boy played the role of an easy meal to perfection. He got the woman's attention by tapping her on the leg, and when she craned her head down to listen , he drew his sawed-off ten-gauge from behind his coat and fired both barrels.

The sound, a tremendous thunderclap, gave the angry mob a start. They all turned from Ptolemy to see Shirley blown half out of her bloody corset. Her face was no longer shimmering porcelain, but it had resorted to its true form—leathery and monstrous.

"Hurry, boy!" Ptolemy yelled over the clamor.

The creature lay flat on its back, flailing about with long curved talons that had once been brightly painted nails. A shrill, inhuman shriek rose from her fanged mouth, cursing in a language unfamiliar to the human ear.

"What the fuck is that?" cried a voice from the mob.

Another cowboy among them wailed, covering his face.

Carson worked fast, straddling the monster's gaping wound as he produced his knife from his belt. He took the creature by its long black hair, pulled it taut, and plunged his knife into its neck.

He sawed the blade back and forth furiously.

"Ah, God," one of the men said, frozen in terror.

The Massacre at Yellow Hill

Mike, the piano player, slumped over into a faint, smashing face-first into the keys. A discordant sound bellowed from the piano just before he hit the floor, out cold.

When the boy finished, the skull came clean away from the neck. Yanking it free of the spine, Carson lost grip of the hair and the momentum sent the bloody head flying into the middle of the watching cowboys. The terrible visage rolled, a long trail of black blood and gore spilling from the stump like a dark ribbon, as the creature's flat, dead eyes, black as midnight, stared at the horrified spectators.

The men shook their heads, as if some strange fog was lifting from their minds.

"That," Ptolemy said, as he shoved the gobsmacked Grouper away from him, "you ignorant pricks, is a vampire."

Every eye in the room turned to look back at Gilbert Ptolemy, who was pulling a whiskey bottle from the mirrored shelves. He turned, jerked the whiskey cork free with his teeth and set the bottle on the bar with a heavy thunk. He spat the cork out onto the ground.

He gazed at them, unflinching. Then said, "I don't know about you boys, but I could sure as shit use a drink."

Chapter Eleven

BIG SPRING, TX

WEDNESDAY HAD BEEN a pretty quiet day, all in all, for Sheriff Roger Smoot. Aside from Willie Masterson getting caught acting a bit too familiar with one of the Lancaster's prize sheep, Big Spring lay as still as a Monday-morning churchyard. He'd spent most of the day cleaning the office rifles, though they'd only been used once a few years back when a man tried to rob the bank with nothing but a note, a block of wood in his pocket, and a sour disposition. A single warning shot was all it took for the robber to fling his hands—and the block of wood—skyward, proclaiming that it had all been one big misunderstanding.

Roger liked cleaning the rifles on slow days. It let his mind wander to places that weren't Big Spring, places where it rained or even snowed. He'd grown up in Kentucky and he missed the blankets of white on crisp January mornings. Big Spring didn't have snow. It had a hot-as-hell season and cold-as-a well digger's ass season. The former was intolerably longer than the latter.

His father, worried that his son would wander through life without purpose, knew a newly elected mayor in a small West Texas town, and wouldn't it be just wonderful if his twenty-five-year-old bachelor son could find a career in serving the public trust? Six years since then—six years without autumn or a woman worth marrying. He wasn't about to go to romancing cloven-footed animals like Willie Masterson, but he did start to wonder how long he could hold out here. Brothels were out of the question too; folks that funded the community chest wouldn't stand for such a waste of the public trust. So, Sheriff Smoot cleaned rifles on slow days, stopped men from unnatural relationships with livestock, and knocked drunks colder than a wedge at the Mustang when they deserved it. Or, sometimes, if he got just plain bored.

He locked the long guns away and had just grabbed his hat and blown out the lights when a knock came at the door.

"Sheriff Smoot? Sherriff, are you there?"

"Shit," he said to himself. That was Martha Primmon. Roger rubbed his brow. If he was real quiet, maybe she'd…

He sighed, thinking better of it, and went to the door. Opened it. "Howdy, Mrs. Primmon."

Sweat rolled down her flushed jowls and soaked her corn-blue dress. "Evening, Sheriff. I have pressing business. I know it's late—

"It's fine, ma'am. What seems to be the problem?"

Martha took a big breath, rolling her eyes and rolling into her story. "A boy rode into town with a man…" She trailed off, puffing harder than a steamboat. "Whew, this town is just getting bigger and bigger."

Roger was sure that the only thing keeping her upright was the straining corset hidden beneath her clothes. He forced that thought out of his mind as quickly as possible.

"Maybe I should ask Michael about getting us a buggy," she said, still puffing.

The Massacre at Yellow Hill

"A boy rode into town with a man…?" Roger said.

"Yes, sir, Sheriff." She lowered her voice to almost a whisper. "A colored man rode into town with a little white Christian boy. No older than twelve, he must have been. Said his parents were dead and that the…the…"

"Man."

"*Colored* man."

"Did the boy seem like he was in danger, Mrs. Primmon?"

Halfway across town, a gunshot split through the evening.

"Oh my good God in Heaven," she said. "He's gone and killed somebody."

She kept talking as Roger hurried back to the gun case, unlocked it, and took out one of the rifles. He took a box of bullets and stuffed them into the loader. The freshly greased hinge snapped cleanly with each new round.

"Please don't get hurt, Roger. And please—please, for Heaven's sake—don't hit that boy. He's as gentle as a dove, I just know it."

He pushed past her, swung his leg over his horse, and squeezed the gelding to a trot.

It made sense that the saloon was the first place to look. God help any black man, toting a white boy or not, who tried to get a drink in the Mustang. The bar owner, Grouper, hated Black people like Cain hated Abel. Roger half expected to feel his heart racing, but, once he dismounted and pulled the rifle free of its sheath, he found that his heart was calm. Mind clear.

Strange thing was, no one had come screaming or streaming out of the saloon into the sunless street, and he hadn't heard a second shot. Rushing up to the swinging doors, his young but deft eye caught a thick ribbon of blood sprayed on the walkway under the lamplight outside the saloon.

He nailed himself against the wall next to the doors and called out, "This is Sheriff Roger Smoot. Jonas, is everyone all right in there?"

"Come on in, Sheriff." Jonas Grouper's voice sounded even more pinched than usual.

Roger leaned out, lifted a wary eye over the top of the doors, and then pushed through, the rifle cradled against his elbow.

What he saw at the bar could have knocked him flat on his back.

A Black man was not only standing behind the bar but by God if he wasn't pouring drinks to the whites. The room was tense with quiet.

Grouper, his face bloodied, stood behind the bar next to the large black man.

"Well," Roger said, as he lowered the rifle. "What the hell is going on in here?"

Grouper put up his hands defensively. "All is calm now, Sheriff. Now I will attest what you're gonna see is pretty shocking."

"That ain't no shit, Jonas. I'm pretty well surprised by the present situation."

Grouper shook his head and gestured his palms down at the floor in attempt to calm the Sheriff. "No, you ain't seen it yet."

It was the way he said it that made Roger's ass clench tight. He didn't like it when folks didn't just shoot straight from the beginning. Holding someone in calculated anxiety was a kind of talk that made him downright pissed. "Well, what the hell is it then?" he barked.

The cowboys shuffled away from the bar. Roger saw what they had been hiding. It was on the floor and it was...well, he couldn't tell what it was, he only knew that he didn't like what he saw. At first glance it looked like a giant coyote head wracked with mange. The skin was too leathery though, and the teeth were long and sharp, but not lined up in a lupine fashion. And there was blood, so much black blood, splashed on the wood floor.

His anger grew hotter. "Somebody better tell me what the fuck is going on and right goddamn now."

Grouper's hands lifted, palms up. A different gesture with the same meaning, trying to calm him. "Sheriff—"

"Put your goddamn hands down, Jonas."

"Sorry," said Grouper, complying. "Look, this here is Gilbert Ptolemy, and, Sheriff, you ain't going to believe what happened in here. Shirley…Shirley was—"

"A vampire, Sheriff," Ptolemy said. The big man moved around the bar toward Roger.

"A what now?"

"A blood-drinking succubus of the night, who I'm guessing has been lying low in this town for months now. I got word of the creature from my man in Abilene, who got word she was working in Louisiana, where she went by the name of Gloria. But make no mistake, it was her. The boy and I," explained Ptolemy, "we work like bounty hunters. Only we look for things like Shirley here. We hunt the enemies of man, not the fools who break man's laws."

"You're telling me that"—he stabbed his rifle at the monstrous head on the ground—"is Shirley? The dancer?"

"We all saw the change happen, Sheriff," Grouper said, wincing as he placed a rag over his busted nose. "Goddamnedest thing you ever did fucking see."

"Shirley. That's fuckin' Shirley," he said, utterly disbelieving and stumbling over his words.

"Everyone has trouble the first time, Sheriff. Provide me with your cable wire and I'll be happy to produce proof of my claim with not just the body but by a sworn statement by Judge Hezekiah Ellison of Abilene in the morning."

"Well, did she kill anybody?" Roger was lost.

"Not here. Not yet. I reckon she was taking her time, trying to hide from any authorities that might come looking for her after she killed a family near New Orleans. Some of your people here tell me that a few of their heifers have gone missing recently. My guess is she was feeding on those to slake her thirst."

Roger's dumbfounded look melted into anger. He focused on Ptolemy. "Beg your pardon, Mr. Ptolemy, but I'm gonna need a little more fucking proof than that."

Ptolemy led the sheriff behind the stage, where Carson, gripping the strange creature's corpse by the fabric of the corset, was rolling it onto a tarpaulin. It flopped over on its back, the ragged neck stump sluicing blood each time the boy pulled its gory bulk.

Roger looked down at the remains of what had, just that morning, been the most beautiful woman in Big Spring. He'd dreamed of Shirley many times before, but he was certain that when he next dreamed of her, it would no longer be the fantasies of a man's lonely mind. It would be of how her hands had transformed into those long curved claws, her swollen breasts flattened like rotted water skins, her sweet smile turned into something wolf-like with wide—much too wide—jaws.

He shook his head.

"I know." Ptolemy said, looking down at the headless corpse. "The first time you see one, you ask yourself how you failed to see it all along. How could something so pleasing be hiding something so terrible?"

The man had sharp features, his muscle thin but corded. The boy had a strangely iron stomach, Roger noticed: he never paused or grew green in the face while handling the bloody mess. They were certainly the couple Martha Primmon had huffed about at the jailhouse.

The Massacre at Yellow Hill

"Reckon you boys been doing this a while."

"We are a unique set, Sheriff. Normally we would have hunted this creature away from the public eye, but once we saw the kind of spell she had over the men, I knew we had to take our action."

Roger smiled at Ptolemy. "Took an awfully big set of balls to walk into a place like this, being as you are."

Ptolemy did not smile back. "Ignorant men don't scare us, do they, Carson?"

The boy, who was just finishing lacing the tarpaulin closed, cinched a final knot taut. He looked at the sheriff with big green eyes. "No, sir. Not one damn bit."

"Bag up the head," Ptolemy told him, then he turned to Roger. "We'll need a small wagon to take the remains outside of town. Sometimes the body burns up against the power of sliver, sometimes not. No clue as to why. We'll burn the body away from the public."

Roger nodded. "I've got one at the jail. Fine by me if you use it, long as you bring it back."

"We're hunters, Sheriff, not thieves." Ptolemy finally smiled.

Roger immediately wished he hadn't. There was no joy in the look, only a cold, cordial meanness.

The wagon was brought to the saloon where under the cover of night, the sheriff helped Ptolemy load the corpse. He did not know why, but he was very careful with the body, setting it down delicately. Ptolemy on the other hand simply dropped his end.

Before they left in the borrowed wagon, Ptolemy addressed all the cowboys, telling them to keep their mouths shut about what they'd seen. He explained to them that Shirley wasn't the only one of her kind and that if another of her ilk found out what had happened, that creature would slash a red line through this city for the sake of revenge.

The boy came out of the saloon holding a leather bag. Roger didn't have to ask what was inside. He wondered what on Earth could have happened in the life of this child to put him in the company of such a strange man with an even stranger profession.

"How'd the two of you team up, son?" asked Roger.

"My father was the same kind of hunter we are. Mr. Ptolemy was his servant. I ride with Mr. Ptolemy now."

"Must be hard, riding with someone like him."

"Mr. Ptolemy is the best man I've ever met. Life ain't so hard for us, 'cept for what men like those cowboys over there make it."

"Well, don't hold it against them. They just don't know any better."

Carson looked over at the cowboys, his eyes narrowing. "I do hold it against them. Mr. Ptolemy says ignorance is a piss-poor excuse for hating someone. He's twice a man as any of them."

Roger nodded. "I believe you."

From the winged doors of the saloon, Ptolemy called the boy. "Body's loaded. Let's go." He looked at Roger, the fire of the lamp light swirling in his brown eyes. "You wire Judge Ellison in Abilene. We'll bring back the wagon in the morning and get what's owed to us."

Roger dipped his hat to him. "Should be done just after breakfast."

Carson and Gilbert Ptolemy walked out together into the night.

It was the last time Roger ever saw them alive.

Chapter Twelve

BIG SPRING, TX

CARSON SAT NEXT to Ptolemy, his head swaying in rhythm with Vanilla's slow, plodding gait. All the stars were out. He hated the Texas heat, but when it came to sunrises and sunsets and wide-open places where a sky could show you all the color of its wealth, well, there was no place he had ever seen do it better. Bright and clean and burning in among the milky white and blackest places in the sky, stars were everywhere. And it was their light that showed Vanilla the powdery road leading out of Big Spring as she pulled the little wagon.

Carson was tired. His eyelids drooped, and fatigue wrapped itself around him like a warm blanket. But each time his eyes closed, his mind assaulted him with the vampire's face, frozen in fanged terror just before the thunder cut her in half.

She hadn't suspected him, and neither had the two before that. What did a creature of such monstrous power have to fear from a small child? He was prey to them. A morsel of a meal. But this particular meal came with a sawed-off ten-gauge filled with silver shot.

His knife had been edged in silver too, and when it touched the skin of the damned, most of the time anyway, it made their flesh sizzle and smoke, sundering the flesh.

Carson had developed a method in his mind to push away such thoughts and visions, but it took time to take full effect. He never 'fell' asleep, but rather it felt to him like he had to climb up a mountain of wakefulness. Up toward rest. Slow and careful and steady to avoid the slippery memories and the blood and the fear that so often sent him falling into terror. It was more like falling awake, he thought. When that method failed, and the horrors of his life sent him tumbling, and his eyes would snap open and, heart racing, he would look for Mr. Ptolemy. Seeing him made things better. And so even now, bumping along the road, the boy's eyes grew heavier and heavier as he made the ascent toward rest.

"Some kind of watchman you are. Fallin' asleep on the job like that," said Ptolemy.

Carson could hear the grin on Ptolemy's face. He leaned his head against the man's shoulder, smiled. "I'm not asleep," he said.

"Well, you've gotta a funny way of looking awake."

Carson laughed and couldn't help but open his eyes. In the light of the oil lamp hanging from an iron hook over the wagon brake, the face of the man he loved so much peered back down at him.

"Sorry, Pa." It felt good to finally say the word. Ptolemy might not have been the man who helped birth him into this world, but there was no question that he was Carson's father now.

Ptolemy slid an arm across the boy's shoulders and squeezed him close. "It's okay, son. The work you did tonight, none of those men in the saloon could have done. You were steady when other folks would have fumbled their gun. I couldn't have done it better myself."

The Massacre at Yellow Hill

Ptolemy squeezed him once, then slid loose from his embrace and took the reins in both hands. "We've got a few miles to go. You kick off to sleep. I'll wake you when it's time for work."

Only the sound of the wagon wheels grinding through the sandy path could be heard among the flat expanse of the desert trail. The boy was asleep now. Ptolemy took his pipe from his jacket pocket along with a long, thin strip of cedar. He clenched the pipe in his teeth, lit the cedar through the slit in the oil lamp, then kissed the flaming tip to the pipe. The thick tendrils of smoke, smelling sweetly of vanilla, puffed out of the bowl in expanding O's.

He smoked and went to a deep place in his mind. A place filled with visions of Carson on that night three years ago. The night they made the pact to be family to one another. A family knitted together in the face of horror.

He remembered the second time he was on the auction block, the Georgian plantation owners examining the whipped, red flesh on his back, buttocks, and thighs. They prodded his mouth with long, thin sticks so as to be sure to not get negro spit on their hands while examining his teeth, saying words they didn't know he understood.

A gaunt man, tall as Ptolemy, was the only one among the whites who looked into his eyes, staring deeply as if searching for a speck of light in Ptolemy's irises.

"Can you read?" the man had asked.

Ptolemy said, "Yes."

At the word, half the crowd laughed. All of them thinking he was a liar.

The gaunt man reached into his breast pocket. "Where did you learn?"

"Man selling me now liked to hear poetry read to him out loud. Made me learn so I could read it for him when he went blind."

The thin man produced a book from his breast pocket. He split the book open, then pointed to a well-worn page. "Show me."

Ptolemy looked down at the book. The words were strangely arranged but he read them all the same. "'But I that am not shaped for sportive tricks,'" he read. "'Nor made to court an amorous looking glass. I that am rudely stamped—'"

The man snatched the book away with a smile. "Excellent. What is your name?"

"Gilbert Ptolemy."

"No doubt your blind master was a lover of history. Well, Gilbert Ptolemy, my name is Ezra Watts, and you'll be coming with me. You might have been born in this godforsaken state into bondage, but you sure as hell won't die that way."

An hour later, in December of 1864, Ezra Watts bought him for one hundred and fifty dollars. A hefty sum but worth every nickel, Ezra had said. And the man's word proved true: it was the last day Ptolemy ever spent in chains. That very afternoon, Ezra replaced the iron manacles with fine clothes, a new pair of boots, and a winter coat. The tailor from which the items were purchased had refused to let Ptolemy step through the door. He did, however, agree to take Ptolemy's measurements on the walkway outside. The coat had served him well, keeping the winter chill out of his bones. Even after three years of use, the garment remained with him always— though he seldom needed it this far south. Sometimes he found himself looking at it as a reminder that whatever Ezra had become in the end, there had once been a measure of kindness in him.

The Massacre at Yellow Hill

A month after that coat's purchase, Ezra had taken Gilbert to a Pennsylvania courthouse to get certified as a free man. Even though Lincoln's proclamation had made all men free, they had the papers drawn up anyway. Ezra's work would take them through the North and South alike, he had said, and getting the papers drawn up was a precautionary measure.

And it was in Pennsylvania that Gilbert Ptolemy met the son of his employer.

The boy that Gilbert had taken as his own

Ezra Watts called himself a researcher of the occult sciences, working for Judge Hezekiah Ellison of Abilene, Texas. He was a man whose profession involved knowing things that men were not meant to know, seeing things they were not intended to see. And its trappings caused men to act in ways no man should ever act.

The wagon rolled over a stone, jostling the lamp. He looked back. The lights of Big Spring had disappeared. Vanilla gave a whinny of appreciation as he called her to a stop.

He patted Carson awake and told him to strike a simple camp while Ptolemy would gather wood for a second fire.

Carson rubbed his sleepy eyes and did as he was told, blearily shuffling among the brambles in the shining starlight where, for a time, Ptolemy stopped among the wind-swayed mesquites to watch. The boy unaware, observed by the man who loved him.

Ptolemy collected the crumbling mesquite littering the ground and bundled together the thick branches. It took a lot of gathering, but eventually he had enough to fashion the timber into a bed of wood set a little distance from their camp. He lifted Shirley's remains, shouldering the tarpaulin, and carried her into the darkness. He set them atop the mesquite and struck the fire to life.

They sat by a small fire near the tent Carson had cobbled together as they watched Shirley's body smolder then take to light.

None of Ezra's writings or books had ever explained why a vampire's body burned with a white flame. A mystery still unsolved to Ptolemy and his adopted son.

"Please don't leave me like that again," Carson said, breaking the silence between them. He was staring at the campfire.

Ptolemy looked at the boy, a freshly loaded pipe clenched in his teeth. "You mean in the saloon? Son, I knew you could handle Shirley."

"What if those men had shot you, Pa? What if the bartender hadn't talked with you but just pulled a revolver?"

The boy's green eyes were glassy.

"I was ready," Ptolemy said.

The boy looked at him. The tears in his eyes weighed heavy as a millstone on Ptolemy's heart.

"I'm not," said Carson.

A heavy, airless silence passed between them.

"Can we please just always do it together?" Carson said. "I always feel better when we do it together."

"I can't promise that, son. Even now, I don't know of a way we could have taken that room without me distracting those men captured in the creature's trance. But," he said, nodding his head, "I will say this though: I'll always try for us to act together. Okay?"

Carson nodded, "I just don't want to lose— "

"You aren't gonna lose me. And I sure as hell ain't going to let anyone take you from me."

The boy pulled his knees to his chest and rubbed his nose against his sleeve. "Okay."

"Get some rest," Ptolemy said. "We'll head back to town in the morning. Get us a big breakfast and put tonight behind us."

The boy got up and hugged the man around the neck, his slender arms clutching as tightly as his frame could afford.

The Massacre at Yellow Hill

"I love you, Pa."

Ptolemy rubbed the back of the boy's head softly. "I love you too, son."

When the boy fell asleep, Ptolemy stared long into the night, worrying on potential calamities as only a father can.

Chapter Thirteen

BIG SPRING, TEXAS

———————

THE MOMENT THEY rode back into Big Spring, Ptolemy knew something was wrong. A mob of folks were rushing along the thoroughfare toward the center of town. That panicked mass lengthened to a stream of people flooded toward the windows the Black Mustang. Peering inside, some cried out at what they saw, and others screamed in horror as they clutched each other.

Ptolemy pulled Vanilla to a stop a hundred feet from the anxious mass. He and Carson dismounted and approached.

Using his bulk, Ptolemy pushed through the press of people so as to look inside.

The smell hit the gunslinger long before he got to the window, though.

The odor of death.

Through the windows of the saloon, he saw what had horrified the townsfolk. Half a dozen men hung from the second-story banister, their rib cages agape, riven open to allow the thick purple ropes of intestines to knot around the railing high above them. Some had their throats torn open. Others had caved-in skulls, as if struck by a cattle maul. Crimson streams had dried on their naked chests and soaked through their boots. A thick swarm of flies buzzed about the exposed entrails. The smell of fresh blood was sharp in the air.

Ptolemy recognized them as the men who had been under Shirley's thrall, the cowboys that had drank with him after the vampire had been destroyed. Each of them laid out in horrific display such as he'd never seen.

Wives of the cowboys cried out to God—the prayer of freshly made widows, asking the uniquely human question of why. Friends of the newly widowed women tried to console them, ushering them away from the ghastly sight. This opened a lane through the press of onlookers into the Mustang for Ptolemy and Carson. The boy followed his father inside.

The saloon's owner, Jonas Grouper, lay on his back over the bar, the dark walnut now stained black by what had been done to him. His throat had been shorn wide. Three ragged lines opened so wide and deep that Ptolemy could have counted the vertebrae comprising the spine. His bottom jaw was missing, torn away. A thick, pulpy mass of tongue lay like a fat slug over the ruin of his throat.

"Aye, God," escaped Ptolemy's lips. Turning from Grouper, he scanned the rest of the place.

Across the saloon, broken ivory keys littered the ground leading to the piano. The instrument, broken down the center, slouched. Two legs bent awkwardly from the cabinet, sticking out of the top of the piano stack. Likely the piano player Grouper had called Mike.

Scanning further to his left, he saw the young Sheriff Roger Smoot. His guts were hanging over his belly and crotch, and the top half of his skull cap had been torn open. The exposed brain, slick with blood, was angled in the morning light, giving it the appearance of overcooked sofkee. In the place where his heart should have rested, there was a sheet of paper dangling inside the cavity on a thin cylinder of wood.

Ptolemy walked over to the sheriff's body, leaned down, and jerked the note free from the wood impaling Roger's chest and keeping him upright.

He looked at the note for a long time.

It read:

> The Waterson child and his companion are to be left inside the saloon by moonrise. Capture them for me or I will return each night, like a plague, and mark this town under my pestilence. You have never known a wrath such as mine.
> —*Sigurd of Antioch*

"Pa," Carson said, giving no mind if someone heard him. "What does it say?"

Ptolemy stood up and walked back over to his son. He handed the note to Carson. "We need to get out of here."

"Sigurd of Antioch?" asked Carson.

Ptolemy headed for the saloon doors. "Come on!" he said. "We need to tell Judge Ellison what's happened."

They trod back over to the wagon and drove it to the sheriff's office. As Ptolemy had suspected, the door was unlocked, and the office was empty. They went in, locked the door behind them, and drew the shades down.

"Before I wire, let me see the note." He snatched it from Carson and read it again.

"Do you think anyone else read it?" Carson asked quietly.

Ptolemy lit his pipe and read it again. "I do not. It also appears that Grouper gave this Sigurd of Antioch the false name you used."

"So, what do we do?"

At that moment, the boy looked so young to Ptolemy, so shaken and frail. His hands were laced in his lap, clenched together tightly so as not to shake. He wanted to tell his son not to be afraid, that everything was going to be okay. They had killed vampires before. But they had always been the hunters, never the prey. The element of surprise had proven the best tactic against the superior speed, strength, and viciousness of such creatures.

"We can't run and leave these people to die," Ptolemy said, "and there is no way we can convince them to leave. Besides, Sigurd would hunt them down and slaughter them in the night. Aside from that, I doubt they'd believe us without evidence. We destroyed that last night."

"We could wait for him inside the saloon, Pa. When he shows up, we could take him by surprise, just like we've done the others."

Sweet-smelling smoke danced all around the man's face as he shook his head. "This ain't like the others, son. We have no advantage. You've seen how quickly they move and how strong they are. If we open fire and miss, he'll be on us, and it will be over quicker than it began."

"Can you track him, like you did in Mississippi with that one that was killing those folks at the plantation?"

Ptolemy held the smoking pipe in his hand, considering. "Tracking an animal such as this is possible when there is high growth, grass and thick trees for them to leave a sign of path. Out here, there's nothing to follow. It's all sand and mesquite. Any trace is blown away within an hour of it first being made. The likelihood of finding Sigurd's lair—"

"We gotta try, Pa. Else he's gonna come back here and...and—"

A shuffling noise came from down the hallway that led to the cells.

The Massacre at Yellow Hill

Ptolemy and Carson eyed each other. In unison, they jerked their weapons from their holsters and pointed them toward the short hall. The jail only held two cells, the set of barred doors both hung open.

"We hear you down there. Make yourself known!" Ptolemy pulled back the heavy hammer on his Walker Colt.

A man's voice came from one of the cells: "I don't want no trouble."

"You armed?"

"Damn right I am."

"Well, we mean you no harm, so long as you mean the same to us."

"I was in the saloon last night. I saw what happened to those poor bastards. You put down those guns and I tell you all I seen."

"You first," Carson said.

Ptolemy nodded at the boy.

After a moment, a long sigh came from one of the cells. Then a revolver came flipping end over end, clattering next to Carson. The father and son looked at the gun on the ground. Ptolemy lifted his chin silently at the boy.

Carson picked the gun up, careful not to give any indication that he now held it in his hands.

"All right, now lemme hear those guns hit the ground." The man called from his hidden place.

Carson dropped the revolver, then waited half a second to drop his own sawed-off shotgun to the floor. All the while, Ptolemy kept his big Walker Colt pointed down the hallway.

"Okay, I'm coming out."

He wore the garb of a dusty miner, his wrinkled brown hat bleached by the sun and sweat, brightening the crown to an al-most tan color. The man was a Mexican with dark brown skin and his thin mustache upon his face turned low when he saw the Colt pointed at him.

"Well, shit," he said, lifting his hands into the air.

"Turn around," Ptolemy commanded.

He complied.

Holding the gun in his left hand, Ptolemy searched the man with his right. He didn't find anything other weapons, so he holstered his own gun. "Okay, hands down. Just had to make sure you were being level with us."

"Can I get my iron back?" He was looking at the boy, who had holstered his own gun and was now holding the revolver.

"No," Ptolemy said, "but you can have it back after you tell us what you saw and are on your way out of town."

The man stared. They were eyes Ptolemy knew, the gaze of a man who had taken orders his whole life and was just about ready to lash out at the next person who tried to tell him what to do. He eyed Ptolemy hard and then, like most men who tried to stare through Gilbert Ptolemy, he cowed, letting his eyes fall away.

Ptolemy led the man back to the office area and offered him one of the chairs next to a big oak desk. "What's your name?"

"Lucas Ramos. Who the hell are you?"

"I'm Gilbert Ptolemy, and this here is Carson."

Carson tipped his hat, saying nothing.

"When were you at the saloon last night?" Ptolemy said, perching himself on the edge of the dead sheriff's desk.

"After you and the boy had gotten done with your business, I figure. I come from a little town, Yellow Hill, and I rode out of there to get away from just about the weirdest shit I've ever seen or heard. Well, right up until last night. Come to find out I spent a week on a horse, in the middle of the godforsaken desert, just to end up watching seven men get their guts pulled out by some dandy-looking fuck in a long cape-coat. Just like in Yellow Hill," he said, drifting for a moment on the thought. "I rode in, paid for a night in the saloon with the last bit of cash on me, seeing as I left my previous terrible fucking situation without collecting my wages. I was in my room upstairs, getting ready to bunk down for the night, when the piano music and general conversation went quiet. I cracked open my door and looked out through the slit. I could see a fella, 'bout as tall as you but thin. I mean thin as the edge of a knife. He had long, curly black hair and as pale as they come," he said. "The bartender kept asking if he could help him or if something was the matter, but he just kept quiet. Eyeing the crowd like a wolf circling a wounded calf. Man wearing a sheriff's tin walked over to him, all friendly like, and asked if something was wrong. That's when it all went to shit. He snatched that sheriff up by the neck with one goddamned hand. Picked him up off the ground and hit him so hard with his other that half his teeth came flying out of his mouth."

Ptolemy shook his head, "And I'm guessing folks drew their guns in defense."

Carson swallowed hard.

"Naturally, some of the cowboys drew their revolvers and went to shooting. The bar filled with gun smoke like the place was on fire. Well, the very second I saw one of those bullets drill a hole through the dandy's chest, and it didn't do nothing but piss him off further, I got my shit right then. Slipped out the window in my room and climbed down into the street. I wanted no fucking part of that fight. Figured the safest place to hide would be where no one would come looking. No reason to head to a jailhouse if your sheriff got his melon smashed in. Got too scared to go back for my horse and tack, so slept here. Thought I'd wait for shit to blow over. Then you boys showed up and I heard you say you're the reason for all this town's bad fortune?"

"The creature calls itself Sigurd," Ptolemy said. "He is going back to the saloon tonight, and if the boy and I are not there waiting for him, he will likely slaughter the entire town, men and women and children all, as a reckoning for what happened to his fellow vampire."

"Vampire? What the fuck is a vampire?"

"A creature of the night," Carson said. "One who drains the blood of the living so as to sustain its immortality and unnatural power."

Ptolemy nodded. The boy had quoted Ezra's writings verbatim. "They are a plague on the world, Lucas," he said. "Very few people know about them, but we do. Our trade is in the eradication of vampires and other creatures of malevolent, predatory power."

Lucas stood and rubbed his sweaty palms on his britches. "Well, boys, I wish you all the luck in the world, but as for me, I'm headed to prairies further fucking north."

"Hold on," Carson said. "You said you saw something weird in Yellow Hill. Was it something like the vampire?"

Lucas turned to him. "Bright boy. But what I saw there wasn't nothing like a vampire, something else. Something I have no wish to describe. I shouldn't have mentioned it, seeing as I'm trying to get the hell away from that too. Mr. Ptolemy, I'll take my gun back now."

"Slow down there, Ramos. There are a few things still left to discuss."

"Like hell there are."

"I wouldn't try to tell a man that he isn't free to go where he pleases and when he wishes to do so, but you have seen the vampire in action. That makes you perfect to help us kill the thing."

Lucas shook his head violently. "Not just no, but hell no. I watched half a dozen men throw lead at him, and that...thing didn't even blink."

The Massacre at Yellow Hill

"Lead was the problem," said Ptolemy. "Silver can wound a vampire—silver and sunlight—which is why they only hunt at night. Hit them with lead all you want, doesn't faze them one bit. Seeing as Carson and I here can't command the sun, we carry a cache of silver-tipped bullets."

Lucas cocked his head. "That's all fine and goddamn good, but what in the hell is in it for me? Why shouldn't I just ride out of this town like I did Yellow Hill?"

Ptolemy stared Lucas in the eyes, and an unspoken contest of wills waged between the two men. "You said you left Yellow Hill with little cash, yes?" he asked, but didn't give Lucas a chance to respond. "Carson, here's your arithmetic lesson of the day. How much money did we get paid for bringing in that Mississippi bloodsucker?"

"Five hundred dollars a fang," the boy said.

"Mm-hmm. And how many fangs reside inside a vampire's mouth?"

"Four, sir."

"If you count Shirley and Sigurd, how much are we looking to get paid from Judge Ellison for this here trip to Big Spring?"

Carson narrowed his brow and looked at his hands, his fingers lifting as he counted. "Umm…"

"Four thousand, son. Four thousand dollars."

"Bullshit," Lucas scoffed.

"Half of which I will give to you if you help us. I'll even pay you another fifty dollars to tell me about that weird trouble in Yellow Hill."

Lucas frowned at Ptolemy, the numbers rolling around in his mind like two boulders. "Two thousand and fifty dollars…"

"Even give you your gun back," Ptolemy said with a big grin.

Lucas chuckled to himself gravely, some dark thought crossing his mind. Then his smile turned more serious, a viper's smile. "Looks like I'll be needing me some of those fancy bullets of yours."

Chapter Fourteen

BIG SPRING, TEXAS

THE TOWN LAY quiet the rest of the day. People stayed in their homes to escape the long, rolling heat of the sun. The air was absent of the clang of a blacksmith's hammer and empty from rustling in the livery stable. Only two businesses were open that day, the carpenter and the undertaker, both for the same reason.

One gathered the bodies from the saloon and took their measurements for the other, and the other worked all day to fit those numbers, setting what must have been a personal record for the number of coffins assembled in a day. A lone preacher in a dusty frock coat visited each of the seven widows and their half-orphaned children. Ptolemy spied him from the jailhouse, watching him brave the heat of the day as he walked a lonely path from home to home.

Carson took Vanilla to the back of the jailhouse where, sitting in the shade, the two men and the boy ate a lunch of salted jerky and drank from bloated water skins procured from the bounty hunter's saddlebags. Over the course of eating, Lucas Ramos told them the story of what had happened in Yellow Hill. Told them of Jeremiah

Hart's mine, the tragedy befalling George Miller and Mark Marple, the creatures he had seen. The terror he had witnessed.

"The world is just turning stranger all the time," Lucas said. "I mean to get away from it after I get my money."

"You'll get paid," said Ptolemy. "If you do things our way."

They planned against the vampire all the early afternoon, then each of them took rest to prepare for a long night.

The plan was simple: Ptolemy and Carson would wait inside the saloon at the table farthest from the door, while Lucas would hide on the second floor, prone and hidden on the open balcony with one of the rifles they took from the sheriff's gun cabinet. When the creature came in, Lucas would fire the first shot. With the vampire stunned, they would all let loose in a hail of gunfire. Ptolemy would then go in for the killing stroke.

In Ptolemy's experience, vampires were more predators than strategists, acting on their base instincts rather than calm, measured tactics. That was how they'd killed those that had come before. And it would be, Ptolemy thought, how they'd end Sigurd.

They walked through the empty town just as the sun was setting. The Black Mustang was empty, silent, and dark. They lit all the lamps on the first floor, bathing the saloon in a pyrite glow. The carrion stench remained oppressive.

Ptolemy walked over to the blood-stained bar and grabbed a bottle of whiskey.

"You're sure you don't want me to aim for the head?" Lucas asked.

"Can't be sure you'll hit him with a shot like that. Aim for the chest or guts. Once you start, don't let up. Just keep pumping bullets till your eight shots are done. If he's still standing after that, drop the rifle and pull your revolver."

Ptolemy watched Carson check the shells in his ten-gauge. "Still loaded?" he asked.

The Massacre at Yellow Hill

Carson snapped the gun shut. "You're the one that says always to check," said the boy and set the shotgun on the table nearest the platform where Shirley, only the night before, had enchanted the cowboys in her dark embrace.

"Yes I do," said Ptolemy.

The boy sat down and took a deep breath.

Ptolemy came over with the whiskey bottle, two glasses pinched in his fingers. He set all three down on the table and turned to Lucas. "Head upstairs now," said Ptolemy. "And by God, don't miss."

Lucas nodded and extended his hand to the bounty hunter. Ptolemy shook it. "I won't," he said. Then he headed up the stairs, melting into the shadows of the second story.

Ptolemy sat down next to his son. "Figure now is as good of a time as any to learn you a little bit about whiskey drinking."

"Now?" The boy's eyes could have swallowed silver dollars.

Ptolemy nodded. "Life ain't about waiting on the bad to get here. It's about enjoying every precious moment before the bad shows up and pressing forward after it arrives."

The bottle made a hollow thunk when Ptolemy pulled the cork free. Without spilling a drop, he tipped the bottle, letting the honey-comb-colored liquid fill a glass.

"This is bourbon. It comes from Kentucky."

"So we aren't having whiskey?" asked Carson.

"Best to think of it like this: all bourbon is whiskey, but not all whiskey is bourbon. It's sweeter than rye, which is what most of the folks 'round here drink. We're lucky the late Mr. Grouper had some in his stock."

Ptolemy filled the other glass and slid it over to Carson. "Fellas who drink rye drink it hard and quick because it's harsher than a mouthful of pepper. Rye is the drink of the uncivilized. Gentlemen, such as we are, sip bourbon."

The boy lifted his glass, only to have Ptolemy halt him by cupping a hand over his wrist. "You always toast first, son."

"Toast?"

"Something you say to commemorate an occasion. Like for us, we'd give a toast of thankfulness."

"Like a prayer?"

Ptolemy squeezed the boy's arm gently, reassuring. "Sure. Just like a prayer, except a toast is for people and prayer is for God. Why don't you do the honors?" He squeezed the boy's arm, then lifted his own glass. "Go ahead. You start with Here's to—"

Carson furrowed his brow. "Here's to...umm. Umm." His eyes fluttered wide. "Here's to not getting killed!"

Ptolemy chuckled. "Well, I've certainly toasted to worse things. Now, you touch glasses."

The whiskey glasses clinked together.

"And you drink." He sipped the bourbon, and his son followed suit.

The boy smiled. Then his eyes became glassy, and finally he hacked a cough.

Ptolemy swatted him on the back, laughing. "That good, huh?"

Carson tried to talk, but he coughed a laugh instead. Rubbing the wetness from his eyes, his smile shining in the lamplight. "I think I like beer more."

"Give it time, so—"

A wind, as strong as the force of a thunderstorm, crashed into the front of the saloon, blowing the batwing doors almost off their hinges. The windows cracked, turning to glassy spider webs.

Carson went for his gun, but Ptolemy popped the flat of his palm against the boy's chest.

The winged doors rebounded off the wall and swung open. The empty street was all either of them could see. When they flapped

The Massacre at Yellow Hill

again, a tall figure stood just outside the frame of the door. A thick cloud pooled around his feet, as if the mist were born out of the long, black duster the man was wearing. The crisp, wet smell of a rainstorm ready to break cut the stench of the bar-turned-slaughterhouse.

"Murderers." The word, no louder than a whisper, did not touch their ears but lay directly upon their minds, like fingertips drawn directly across their brain. The creature then pulled open his duster, revealing a single revolver belted at his waist as he reached into an unseen place. He produced something Ptolemy could not make out.

Cloaked in darkness, wreathed in mist, the creature tossed the object into the saloon where it clattered to the floor. A single charred piece of bone lined with carnivore teeth. There were gaps in the jaw where Carson had removed Shirley's fangs only that morning.

A single finger, taloned by a glimmering black nail, pointed at Carson. "The sheriff wouldn't speak your name, even when I began to unravel him. The bartender, though, he was more easily persuaded."

"You must be Sigurd," said Ptolemy. "Come into the light if you're going to stake your claim on us." Ptolemy narrowed his eyes, even though he could feel his knees aching to knock together.

"Your kind knew her as Shirley," said Sigurd, ignoring Ptolemy's demand. "That was not her name. She was Abelia, born in Judah as one of you. Born again in the place called Rome as my eternal bride, swine."

Ptolemy's mind rolled, considering how he might get the creature to enter the saloon so Lucas could take his shot.

"I do not fear your false light." Sigurd's voice burrowed into their ears like a rushing locomotive. The vampire, broad and pale-skinned, moved with such a predatory lope that he seemed to float rather than walk. The heavy mist rolled into the room with him, spilling out like a steamy wave over the floorboards. "Nor do I hold fear of your human weapons. For I am a knight eternal, Sigurd of Antioch, a Templar at twenty-two, reborn by the Vampire King and thus made ageless. I am the most fearsome hand of a ferocious order."

Ptolemy stared into Sigurd's dark, forever-void eyes, a malevolent power radiating off him; a cold star chewing through all heat, strength, and life. The man's lungs strained against the unseen force. Half-breaths were all he could muster. But he did not look away, all the same. Ptolemy had never looked away; his was an iron resolve that had been cast upon the anvil many times before, and never had it broken.

Goddamn it, why hasn't Lucas taken the shot? he thought.

Why am I not shooting? Why isn't Carson—

It took a great measure of strength for him to turn his gaze to Carson. The boy was trembling violently, like an epileptic struggling to restrain an episode. Tears streamed down his face. Ptolemy had only ever once seen Carson react with such fear, years ago during the events that led to his father's death.

Sigurd's sheer presence pressed against them so mightily that Ptolemy felt his spine pressing into the cool wood of the chair. He strained hard, trying to reach for his guns. Trying to move…move anything. He drew in a great breath, then blew out the air from his lungs, spraying spit all over his face. Groaning, he brought forth all his strength. His fingers twitched but refused his command. His teeth began to grind together as Sigurd floated closer, the force so strong he could hear the crowns grating roughly against each other.

From out of the shade of Sigurd's form, a clawed hand unfurled, reaching. The sharpness of those black talons glimmered like molasses in lamplight.

"Now, child," Sigurd said, "I am going to open your belly and feed you whatever I find inside." He was only a foot away from Carson, the nails on his hand so sharp that Ptolemy could see their edges were beveled like razors.

The Massacre at Yellow Hill

Concentrate! *Snap Lucas out of this trance. Snap your own damn self out of the trance!* he screamed inside his own mind.

Ptolemy focused all his effort, all his mind, on one word: a word that all humankind had known since mankind had conquered the world. The thing which, in Ptolemy's experience, had never failed to do harm upon the unnatural horrors he and his adopted son had fought against. He filled his lungs with a wet inhalation, and he screamed.

"Fire!"

Sigurd's head snapped over to Ptolemy, eyes wide and terrible. Then his gaze flew up to the banister of the second story. Flaring his impossibly long fangs, he loosed a reptilian hiss.

Thunder split the night as Lucas fired.

A single red ribbon of blood sprouted from Sigurd's chest.

The vampire roared in fury.

The lever action on the rifle blistered the air, click-clack. Another round laced through the air, boring through Sigurd's shoulder, sending him spinning. The creature took to the air, leaping from the ground like a frightened cat. He planted his claws high up on the wall opposite the banister and opened wide his terrible mouth in rage.

Gilbert Ptolemy then didn't quite understand what he saw next, until he understood it entirely. Like nothing he had ever seen before, like no vampire he had encountered, from beneath the black shoulders of Sigurd's cape-coat flared a pair of leathery wings, flapping violently. The gusts of wind sent chairs and tables clattering all over the saloon. A wind so powerful it blasted Ptolemy's hat off his head and dried his tongue to sandpaper. Ptolemy grabbed for the hat as it flew from him.

Suddenly realizing he was free of Sigurd's influence, a snarl curled across his face. His trained hand blurred for the Walker Colt at his hip. He fanned the hammer, hard and quick. Three shots blasted a smoky cacophony through the saloon. The first two shots drilled holes through the vampire's furious wings, and the third hit the monster in the hand, bursting through his palm and shattering three taloned fingers.

Wounded, Sigurd howled and pushed off the wall. The strength of the leap was so powerful that the timbers of the exterior wall beneath him buckled. Like a mountain lion, he soared across the saloon, his limbs fully extended. Ptolemy fired his last three shots, but couldn't be sure any of them had found their target.

Pieces of the wood banister rained down on the table in front of Ptolemy and Carson, who had only just regained his wits and was picking up his sawed-off ten-gauge.

"Come on!" Ptolemy hollered.

The boy followed him across the room to the stairs.

On the unseen second story, Lucas's rifle fired again, again, and again, the sharpshooter's screams bellowing with each click-clack of the saddle gun's lever action.

His heart pounding, Ptolemy broke his revolver cylinder out of the gun, dumped the spent casings, and reloaded without ever looking at the revolver. He kept his eyes focused on the stairs—on the vampire. At the top of the flight, Sigurd held Lucas by the throat. The man's rifle was now in the vampire's other hand. The vampire lifted the gun by the barrel and smashed the stock into the floor, shattering it into splinters.

Ptolemy screamed, "No!"

Lucas's back faced him, a barrier between Ptolemy and Sigurd, hiding the vampire from clear shot.

In one fluid motion, Sigurd drew the stump of the rifle back. The twisted iron and jagged wood stock came forward, bursting

The Massacre at Yellow Hill

through Lucas's back. A hot spray of blood veiled the air, flying clear across the room and spattering Ptolemy's face.

Lucas screamed and kicked and wailed. Sigurd flung the man over what was left of the banister, sending him crashing onto one of the tables below.

Sigurd roared again, his jaws opening like a snake in mid-strike.

"Now!" Ptolemy ordered. Father and son set their guns to work. revolver and shotgun blasting forth, making war on this creature of immeasurable power.

Ptolemy's revolver drilled the beast, but it was Carson's sawed-off shotgun that staggered Sigurd so mightily that it sent the vampire to his knees.

Sigurd twisted, one of his leathery wings slashing out and catching Carson on the crown of his head, slamming the boy against the wall with a resounding crack. The boy fell slack, then tumbled down the stairs.

Now it was Ptolemy who roared, tossing his empty revolver to the ground as he rushed the wounded vampire. His hand went for his big silver-edged knife.

A quick slashing claw swooped over his head as he ducked and barreled into the vampire's shadowy depths.

He stabbed, plunging the knife deep, over and over and over, feeling the creature's strength wane with each deep thrust.

Sigurd took hold of him at the shoulders. Even with his power diminished, Ptolemy had never been seized by such strength. The monster opened its mouth and reared its head back, ready to sink its fangs into Ptolemy's skull, but Ptolemy turned his knife blade and thrust upward with all his might. His strength and Sigurd's force collided, sending the silver tip of the knife through the left side of the monster's chest. He felt the vampire's fangs collide with the flat of his scalp and drag a hot line across his brow. The world flashed white.

Blood flooded over Ptolemy's eyes.

Sigurd, the knife still embedded in his chest, tossed him across the upper floor. Ptolemy was at once weightless, flying. Then he collided with the wall next to the stairs, the impact sending all the air from his lungs.

He lay on the hard wood floor. *Get up, move, goddamn you*, he said to himself. But when he tried to rise, his boot twisted underneath him, his ankle giving way under his weight with a loud pop.

Weaponless, Ptolemy looked up to see Sigurd taking heaving breaths with dark blood oozing from his many wounds. The vampire whirled around, those predatory eyes searching wildly trying to decide whether he would risk further engagement. The bounty hunter was out of weapons, out of breath, out of time. Ptolemy was of little threat, even with Sigurd greatly wounded, but the vampire didn't know that. He could see the caution in the monster's eyes, his will teetering on the precipice action.He saw the calculation. The fear. It was all Ptolemy could do to save his own life, so, he bluffed. He pushed up from the floor and reached behind his coat, as though he held a secondary revolver at the back of his gun belt.

"Run, you son of a bitch. You know I'm dangerous. Run," Ptolemy thought, begging with the creature.

Sigurd hissed, bringing himself to his full height, wings stretching wide as the balcony where they stood. Then he turned and burst out through the second-story window, flapping his giant black wings as he flew into the starry night over Big Spring.

Ptolemy, exhausted, lifted his head and tried to rise. He had to check on Carson. Had to make sure the boy was all right. Had to keep the promise he had made to him. As soon as his head came higher than his chest, everything in his vision melted to white foam, and then to darkness.

Chapter Fifteen

BIG SPRING, TEXAS

——————

CARSON SWAM THROUGH a bloody river of time, where on the banks squat the myriad of nightmare creatures he and Ptolemy had hunted in their years together. Monstrous claws glimmered with a pale blue moonlight. Their wet fangs dripped with gore, each of them growling or screaming so loudly it threatened to burst the boy's eardrums.

The river washed him around a horseshoe-shaped embankment where a starless void domed the sky. He played possum in the slow drift and hoped none of the monsters realized he was alive. If they did, he knew they would come sloshing into the red river, giving chase through the waters that carried him to the unknown. In his heart he knew if they found him, they would slowly peel open his flesh. And over the sound of his screaming they would eat him. There would be nothing to stop them.

Past the bend of the shoe, a green obelisk rose into view, tall as a windmill and thick as a wagon. The plinth glowed with a strange light, a pulsing luminosity growing brighter and brighter as he drifted toward it.

He knew what was going to happen next. This was a familiar nightmare born of harsh memory. It played out exactly as before. Suddenly, he was on the riverbank, tied down in front of the throbbing light. Ezra, his father, stood over him, his maniac glare open so wide the older man's eyes bulged from their sockets. The black tome was clutched in one hand, a heavy stone in the other. A stone meant for Carson's skull.

The stone, raised high in Ezra's hand, began to fall. A gunshot rang out. Something splashed across Carson's face.

He woke up screaming, howling out of his nightmare at the blurry face of a bearded man he'd never met.

"Jesus Christ," the man shrieked as he fell flat on his rear.

Panicked, Carson swung his vision around the saloon. Behind the bearded man were the faces of half a dozen other men, a few of them clutching shotguns close to their chest. Fear had frozen each of them.

Lucas Ramos was propped up against a wall nearby, his eyes open, looking down at the metal barrel of the rifle protruding from his belly. Carson went to rise, but the world spun and his head felt hot and swollen. He touched the epicenter of the pain and winced. His fingertips came back gritty and wet with crusted blood. The world spun again, and his knees started to give.

"Easy there, son." The bearded man took Carson by the shoulders and kept him upright. "Easy. Everything is going to be okay."

Carson looked at the man sideways. "Let go."

The man lurched back in surprise, then released him.

"Carson?" said Lucas, the man's voice was weak.

Carson rose, slower this time and stumbled to the wounded man.

Lucas lifted his eyes to the boy. And there, in those eyes, like in the nightmare, Carson saw a familiar look. Lucas didn't speak

The Massacre at Yellow Hill

on the finality of his situation; it was an understood truth between them.

"Where—" Lucas shivered with pain. "Where is your pa? Did he kill it?"

Carson swung his head around, his panic returning. He didn't see his father anywhere. Unsteadily, he climbed the stairs, calling, "Pa? Pa!"

Nothing.

On the second floor, at the far end of the hallway, a warm breeze rushed through the shattered glass of the window overlooking the alleyway. Shards lay scattered upon the floor.

"No," he whispered, knowing that the worst had happened. He stumbled toward the broken window, the sharp remnants of glass in the frame were stained with dried, black blood. "Pa!" Carson hollered. Even before he reached the window, he knew what he would find when he looked out: the broken body of his adopted father below.

"Carson," the low voice came from behind him.

At the sound of that voice the whole world tilted. And the boy turned.

Standing on one foot, propped against the opposite end of the hall, was Gilbert Ptolemy. His dark face gray as ash. His head hung low as if he were a traveler who had reached the end of some long journey. "Are you alright, son?"

Carson's heart began to rush. He stumbled first, almost falling, but his feet found their strength and he ran to his father, bounding across the baseboards until the father and son collided. A wet mess of blood and worry, tears, and relief. He clutched the man's neck so tightly it almost choked him.

"It's okay," said Ptolemy.

Carson squeezed tighter.

"It's okay, now. Quit squeezing or you're bound to finish what Sigurd started."

Carson squeezed again, then drew back. Vision blurry with tears, lips trembling, he said, "Please. Please be okay."

"I'm okay, and it's okay. It's okay, I promise."

Carson pulled his face away from his father's cheek. "Mr. Ramos, he's…he's hurt really bad, Pa."

Gingerly, Ptolemy and son made their way downstairs. There, they found the group of men who had wandered into the saloon standing around Lucas with their hands raised in the air.

Lucas was pointing his revolver at them. "Anyone else who comes near me to try and render assistance will be shot through the head. I have lived my life without the pity of white men, and I choose to die that way." He waved his gun at the men. "Ptolemy, tell these men to get back, or so help me—"

"You men step back now," Ptolemy said. "You heard him."

The crowd did as they were told. Ptolemy and Carson went to the dying man, a dark shadow pooled on the floor around him.

"It's a damn shame, Lucas," Ptolemy said. "For what it's worth, we wouldn't have survived without you."

Lucas eyed him hard. "Did you kill it?"

Ptolemy sighed. "Not this time. But we'll find him."

"Well, kill that son of a bitch for me, the next time you see him. And after you do, I want you to go to Yellow Hill."

"Yellow Hill," said Ptolemy.

"I should have stopped things from the beginning. The very night I was standing in that parlor, I could have stopped Hart, but I didn't. You've got to help them. I couldn't. But you…even your boy. You can." He struggled to inhale, working hard for so little a breath. "And that money you owe me for them teeth, the money you promised, that's what I'm using to buy your services."

His voice began to ebb as dark blood ran from the corner of his sun-blistered lips. "I ran—" A heavy breath rattled from his throat.

Lucas Ramos was gone.

Ptolemy shook his head and closed his eyes.

The men behind them, clutched together like frightened hens, took a step forward. Ptolemy swung his eyes around to meet them.

One of the townsfolk, a short tree stump of a man with a black mop of hair, said, "What in the hell happened in here?"

Carson looked at Ptolemy, who let out a deep sigh. Neither of them knew where to start.

But, as was his way, Gilbert Ptolemy opened his mouth and explained the situation. Carson listened, hearing the patient speech of a man who had learned the subtle, hazardous art of calming the fears of White people. Chief among the instruments of that art was speaking slowly, always carefully, and, of course, carrying a letter of authority from Judge Hezekiah Ellison deeming Gilbert Ptolemy and Officer of the Court.

The bearded man was Bill Morris, the town undertaker. He swore to give Lucas a coffin and proper burial at no charge, which, as things went among White men, was the best a dead Mexican was going to get in Big Spring.

"We have need of your wire and a place to hold up and rest," said Ptolemy to Bill. "Will you let the boy and I make use of your late sheriff's office? You have my word we will make no further trouble for you or the rest of the townsfolk."

Several of the men raised their voices in opposition.

Bill quickly cut them off. "If the offices can't be used, perhaps one of you men would rather open their home and hospitality to this man and child?"

When no one piped up, he turned to Ptolemy and said, "There, that's settled then."

Ptolemy had just finished wiring the Judge from the sheriff's office, explaining what had happened and asking him to wire back around two that afternoon, when Bill Morris's wife showed-up with breakfast. Clad in a white sundress, she shuffled about the desk laying out the food for them, and smiled kindly though spoke little .

They ate fresh biscuits and overcooked bacon and drank water until their bellies ached. Then, they slept on a cell cot together, Ptolemy's arm draped over his son.

Ptolemy drifted in and out of sleep, checking his pocket watch every so often to ensure he didn't miss the incoming wire. He stroked the boy's hair between naps and held him close as he examined the gash along his brow. Eight inches lower and his throat would have been ripped to pieces. Ptolemy had never been so grateful for such a short distance.

At 1:30 p.m., Ptolemy slipped out of the cell and limped his way down the hall to the telegraph. His ankle was swollen badly, though he did not think it was broken, and his brain pulsed with a dull heat. He smoked his pipe and chewed at what was left of the bacon, leaving a few strips for the boy for when he woke.

It was 1:55 when the telegraph began to chirp. Ptolemy, who'd waited with a pencil in hand, wrote the message down. Then he took the jumble of nonsense letters through a cipher the Judge had taught him.

The Massacre at Yellow Hill

To: Gilbert Ptolemy

From: Judge H. Ellison

YOUR NEWS IS DISTURBING. NO KNOW-
LEDGE OF VAMPIRE MONARCHY OR ORDER OF
KNIGHTS. HART MAY HAVE CONNECTION TO
SOCIETY OF PROMETHEUS. WILL WIRE PROF.
BASS. PROCEED WITH GREAT CAUTION. WIRE
WHEN YOU REACH YELLOW HILL.

—H.E.

The Society of Prometheus.

"Son of a bitch." Ptolemy crumpled the deciphered note in his hand.

"What's the matter, Pa?" Carson looked thin and ragged in the early afternoon light. Plodding out of the shadow of the hallway, he sat in the chair next to the desk. "That the wire from Judge Ellison?"

"It is."

"Well, what is it?"

"You remember when I was all shot up outside the church where your daddy made all those bad choices. The choices that weren't your fault or mine?"

The smirk drifted off Carson's face as if a gentle breeze had come by and stolen it from him. "Yes."

"I made my promises, and you made yours."

"Yes."

"Told you I'd never lie to you."

"Pa, please tell me what's goin' on."

"I wired the Judge about what Mr. Ramos said about Yellow Hill. He thinks that Mr. Hart might be caught up in the same kind of thing that changed Ezra."

Carson looked down at the floor. "The Society of Prometheus."

Ptolemy nodded. "Your daddy never told us anything about how many there were, or the number of manuscripts drifting out in the world."

"Is the Judge sure?".

"It ain't the Judge's way to guess on such things. He's a man who considers things deeply before he says them. Takes his time with his words."

Carson looked down at his hands. His fingers were laced tightly together, white-knuckled. "Does this mean I have to look in the book again?" He swallowed hard.

Ptolemy placed a hand on the boy's shoulder. "No, son."

"But I'm the only one who can read the language." His breathing grew heavy.

The look of desperate helplessness Carson gave him shattered his heart. It was the pain of paternal betrayal that only a child could know, a pain that would grow as the boy grew. A pain that the child, even as a man, would never forget.

"That book is poison, Carson. I'll never ask you to dare its contents."

Carson nodded, his fingers released their clasp. "So, we're going to Yellow Hill."

"Believe we must."

"What about Sigurd?"

"The society takes priority. Sigurd is a threat to a town; the Prometheus Society is a threat to every town." Ptolemy took a long, hard pull off his pipe. The smoke swirled out of his nose. "I've got a feeling we aren't going to have to find him. When he's good and ready, he'll come looking for us. Vampires have long memories to go with their long lives. We'll need to sleep in shifts from here on out. At least until it's over with him."

The Massacre at Yellow Hill

Carson swallowed hard. "How long will that be?"

"Long as it takes," said Ptolemy. "But I see the worry in you. Don't let that steal your grit; he knows we can hurt him. Knows we're dangerous. Even a bear has to be careful when he decides to take on a pack of wolves."

"Because the wolves are many and the bear is just one."

Ptolemy nodded again. "Exactly."

They found Vanilla in the little stable at the back of the sheriff's office. There were only two stalls. Opposite Vanilla was a well-groomed brown gelding. The late sheriff's horse, no doubt.

"With no sheriff, I reckon we won't be getting paid for our work here, so we'll take the horse, saddle, and rifle in lieu of payment," Ptolemy said. "Besides, it's time you had a horse. You're already too big to be riding with me."

A big toothy grin lifted Carson's face. "You mean?"

"I mean it'll be your job to brush him down, treat his sores, feed him, and learn his gait and posting. Looks like his rigging and tack over there."

Carson found a freshly polished saddle tossed over the side of the stall. It was fixed with a lassoed rope and white sheep's wool ringed the stirrups. He ran his fingers along the slick leather of the saddle. "He really cared for his rig."

"And you'll do his memory a great service by making sure that the leather never cracks and this horse never sees a hungry day."

The boy reached over to the gelding, ran his fingers along the bridge of his nose. The gentle creature pushed back against his hand, guiding Carson's hand along the white star on its forehead.

Ptolemy watched Carson carefully slide his young hands along the horse's spine and hind quarters. The sunlight gave the animal a chestnut glow. The boy's sloping grin revealed him to be filled with a kind of wanderlust afforded to the very young. A reminder that Carson was still so young. Still bearing a small measure of the hopeful innocence that, in time, the world would steal away. The father said nothing, while his boy laid a blue riding blanket over the gelding. Though he was beginning to take a man's length of bone, his face was still smooth as the leather saddle that came next. Carson set the rigging and tack. The gelding whinnied and shied away.

"Easy with him," said Ptolemy. "He doesn't know you yet."

The boy nodded and gently whispered to the gelding as he bridled the horse and asked it to take the bit.

Ptolemy smiled and said nothing else, witnessing the slow, aching transformation of Carson before him. . He just let the boy savor this moment, this fresh gift. He went and put his own tack on Vanilla, taking a moment to mimic the boy and stroke the big mare.

With the gelding fully ready, Carson slipped a foot inside the stirrup and grabbed the saddle horn. But before he could mount, Ptolemy stopped him.

"Hold on now. You're not gonna get on that horse without giving him a name now, are you?"

Carson looked confused.

"Awful bad luck to start off a new friendship without knowing each other's name from the outset," said Ptolemy

"But this was the sheriff's horse. He's already got a name."

"That's his old name from his old life. This is a beginning of a new life...a life with you." He walked Vanilla forward to stand side by side with the horse and his new boy. "You've taken this horse unto yourself, and now you're going to change the kind of life he leads."

"Like when Saul became Paul, after he was blinded by God for all the bad he'd done."

"Mm-hmm."

The Massacre at Yellow Hill

Carson squinted, the mill of his mind grinding over ideas. His eyes popped open in revelation. "Abraham."

"After the president or the patriarch?"

Carson smiled. "Yes."

"It's a good name." Ptolemy leaned over to rub between the gelding's ears. "That all right with you, Abraham?"

The horse shook his head and chuffed a snort.

The boy, remarkably, giggled.

"Well, okay, Abraham," said Ptolemy, "now we're going to Yellow Hill, which is south and further west form here. From what Lucas said, it's a hard trip."

Carson squeezed his heels, guiding the horse out of the stable. "We're up for anything, Pa. Aren't we, Abraham."

Part III

THE MASSACRE AT YELLOW HILL

Chapter Sixteen

YELLOW HILL, TEXAS

THE FUNERAL PROCESSION for Micah Hart marched along the main street of Yellow Hill. Jeremiah, a father in mourning, wore a black suit. A stovepipe hat wobbled on his stooped head as he guided the funeral carriage toward the cemetery. As its black wheels rolled through town, all could see the black sheet covering what was rumored to be a glass coffin through the big circular windows on the sides. Like an army of black ants powdered in sugar, the miners in Hart's employ followed with soot upon their faces and caliche dust upon their clothes. They walked with bowed heads, their hats in their hands.

All the people of Yellow Hill lined the streets, watching the procession. Some to pay respect, but most attending out of fear.

Only the men who had pulled Micah's body from the cave had seen what was left of him. Jeremiah told the men he would pay them double their weekly wages to keep that detail to themselves, and should he hear any utterance otherwise, it would cost those men and their families more than money.

Charlie Gathers rode shotgun next to his employer through the mute parade. The right side of his face was a swollen mass of red and purple, the color of an overripe plum.

Tabitha, Annie, and Georgie Miller stood outside their home, watching as the miners bore Micah a pall fit for a West Texas prince. The Methodists circled together in the cemetery at the burial plot next to a tombstone that read:

Martha Susan Hart
1811–1866
Light of the World - Beloved Mother and Wife

The silent mass waited until the carriage crossed under the iron archway of the cemetery. Normally the voices of the choir were reserved for the graveyard behind the church plot, but as with all things regarding the Hart family in Yellow Hill, an exception was made. As the wheels crossed over the gloomy threshold, the choir began to sing "Crown Him with Many Crowns."

They sang of the creator of the rolling spheres, ineffably sublime, their voices lifted for heavenly trump but mostly lost in a howling wind that ripped beads of sand in their open mouths.

Several rows away, a small mesquite bush had already started to grow near another more recent tombstone that read:

George Robert Miller
1838–1868
Husband and Dutiful Father

Jeremiah Hart, a man now devoid of kin, silently motioned for six of his men to hoist the veiled coffin from the carriage and lower it into the burial plot.

The Massacre at Yellow Hill

Reverend Callum, a slender, bald man ravaged by years in the sun, offered to say a word and blessing upon the recently departed. Mr. Hart rejected the offer with a single upraised palm.

With the mass of miners, the choir, and the reverend standing around the plot, Jeremiah Hart addressed them.

"Here," he said, pointing down at the black veil covering Micah's ravaged body. "Here lies the last measure of what was good in the world. Micah Earle Hart, still a boy, braver than any man among you, tried to do for his father's love what I paid half the men in this town to accomplish." Hart paused, tears in his eyes. "There was so much to tell him. Still so much to say. To reveal."

Hart then looked up and pointed at the multitude of men in his employ. "I blame you. And were it not that I needed your hands for the work ahead…"

Reverend Callum tried to interrupt the grieving father, but a hard stare from Hart screwed him into silence.

"All that is left is the work. Any man who does not show his face at the mine first thing in the morning hazards great peril on himself and his family."

Wide eyed, the audience could only gawk or cast fearful gazes to the freshly dug earth.

"I need to be about my boy," he said. "Leave me to it. All of you." And he took a spade into his thin, weathered hands.

The crowd dispersed. No one among them brave enough say anything, or too afraid or insulted by Hart's words to offer further condolences.

Marty, the old miner who went into the cave with Micah, had not been recovered. All the men had found of him was a gore-spattered boot with the foot still inside.

.

Chapter Seventeen

YELLOW HILL, TEXAS

THAT NIGHT, THE Millers hosted Reverend Gregory Callum over a meager dinner of roasted corn and a beef stew that was mostly carrots and potatoes. Tabitha would have invited Lyle Collins, the president of the diaconate, and his wife, Jessica, but slim provisions prevented a meal larger than Tabitha could afford.

The reverend was a widower and much older than Tabitha, but time and hardship had sapped little of his warmth and none of his cheer. He spoke to the children all through dinner, capturing Georgie's attention with stories of war. Detailing with great rigor his service in the Massachusetts 54th Infantry during the Slaver's Revolt.

Annie picked at her food, the girl mostly bored by the stories of men fighting one another. But the reverend, with his cheerful personality, managed to make her smile when he told a story of President Lincoln visiting their training ground and telling a lewd joke around a campfire.

"A natural storyteller," the reverend said, his eyes wide with remembering. "He once told us that he walked into the middle of a men's wrestling club and let them all know, 'I might appear old to some of you, but make no mistake"—the reverend thinned his voice to impersonate Lincoln—"'I'm the head buck. Anyone thinking of challenging better be prepared to wet your horns.'"

"Did anyone fight him?" Georgie asked, glowing with excitement.

"Not a chance, Junior. He was tall as an elm and strong as a bull. Word and legend is that he never lost a match."

"Is that why Booth shot him?" Annie said, casting a glance into her steaming bowl as she picked at a carrot with her fork.

"Annie Joy Miller," Tabitha chided.

Reverend Callum ignored the rebuke. "That's exactly why the traitor shot him from behind, while he was out with his wife. It is the only fashion by which a coward achieves anything, Annie. Goodness is a light that puts fear into evil men. They know that such a light reveals the true nature of their character, so they act as thieves in the dark. Booth came in the night, like a thief, and robbed all of us of a man of the highest accord."

Annie flicked her eyes from her bowl, flatly staring at the old man. "You killed men, same as him. What makes your killing right and his wrong?"

"Reverend, I am so sorry." Tabitha's tone pierced the air like a needle. "Annie, you are excused to your room."

Reverend Callum's face flushed, but he knew better than to respond.

Annie didn't. "That isn't fair!"

"You are embarrassing yourself and this family. You will go to your room this instant. Your father would be ashamed—"

Annie's mouth broke open, her lips trembling, and she moaned out a cry.

"Now!" Tabitha slapped the table so hard, her spoon flipped out of her bowl, then clattered upon the floor.

The Massacre at Yellow Hill

"Daddy was never ashamed of me!" Annie cried. "He said so!" She burst from the table and ran to her room.

Tabitha grimaced. She jumped when Annie slammed her bedroom door shut. Utterly embarrassed, she tried to apologize to Reverend Callum.

"Children are a blessing that I'm afraid my Betty and I were never gifted," he said. "Please, don't apologize. I shouldn't have pushed my anecdote so far. That was my fault."

Georgie's smile had drooped to a frown. "That was mean, Momma."

"Yes," said Tabitha, setting her head in her hands. "I am very mean, aren't I."

There was a short, heavy silence that filled the house. Tabitha felt all the weight of the quiet in her chest, in her mind, in her very soul. Her ears burned, and her eyes welling with tears. She sniffed.

"Momma?" asked Georgie.

"Yes, sweetheart?" she said, unable to look up.

"I'm sorry we make you so sad."

She looked up at the boy, mouth opening to correct her son. Explain that it was not his fault. But she could not speak. His words were a dagger, slicing deeper than the boy could know.

"Georgie," said the reverend.

Tabitha looked at the man.

"When someone dies, the light they shined on the world dies with them. It goes away. And when it leaves, the world changes. It darkens, because we know that portion of light and its quality will never come back. This is called sorrow. You know this word?"

The boy nodded. "Yes."

"You've felt it with your pa. Your mother feels it. I've felt it too. That dark place where it seems no light can touch."

155

"When your wife died?"

"Yes," said the reverend. "And do you know what helped me work through the loss of my brightest light?

"No."

Reverend Callum leaned close to the boy. "All the other lights around me. All the people who loved me. Even though my wife was gone, those other lights shined bright enough that eventually the darkness of my sorrow became the shadow of my happiness. And from there, following love's illimitable light, I found joy again. You see, Georgie, you and Annie aren't what make your mother sad; you are all the light she can see."

Georgie looked to her, his eyes filling with tears. "I'm going to shine so bright for you, Momma."

Tabitha opened her arms, and Georgie got up from the table and threw himself into them. She smelled his hair, holding him tightly. Kissed him, and they cried together.

"Thank you," she said, looking up at the reverend.

The old man smiled, then looked over to Annie's bedroom door. "Georgie, why don't you and I go outside while your mother and your sister have a chance to talk. I'll show you how to see constellations."

George pulled back from Tabitha, rubbing the wetness from his nose. "Constellations?"

"Think of them like drawings you can see in the stars."

The boy looked at his mother. "Can I?"

She kissed his forehead. "Sure."

When the pair went outside, Tabitha thought about what the old man had said and how she could say the same to Annie. She paused at her closed door, wringing her hands, her stomach knotted with nerves. She took a deep breath and knocked gently, but was met only with silence.

The Massacre at Yellow Hill

"Annie, honey, please open the door. I want to apologize."

Still nothing.

She sighed hard, growing angry that her own daughter wouldn't even give her a chance to say she was sorry. So, she decided to brave the lion's den. "I'm going to come in, sweetheart." She turned the knob and pushed the door open to reveal an empty room. The West Texas wind billowed the curtains about the open window.

Annie was nowhere to be seen.

Chapter Eighteen

YELLOW HILL, TEXAS

THE NIGHT WAS hot. Annie's hair clung to her damp forehead as she fled as fast as her feet would take her. She ran from the hurt. Ran from the words her mother had spoken to her. In her rage, she made a promise that no one would ever talk to her in such a way ever again. It was as if her mother had thrown a stone and shattered her heart into a thousand pieces.

Her blue dress whipped behind her. She was a ghost losing itself in the West Texas wind, a ghost of who she was before her father died. All her future happiness, she believed, had been buried with him.

Cutting through the alley past the main thoroughfare, she found herself in the shadowy locale behind the general store and the saloon. She picked her way between the dark patches of discarded waste that gleamed wet in the lamplight. When she reached a particularly large patch of mud, she extended her stride to leap over it, but missed the landing and fell backward with a yelp. Pain streaked from her ankle all the way up her leg. A sharp acrid stench filled her nose.

In the low light, she brought her hands close to her face, offering her nose a blast of ripe tobacco-spit, urine and feces. The putrid slop from the discarded waste of chamber pots and spittoons was caked to her dress, her hands, and all along her legs.

She tried to stand, but her swollen ankle gave way and she stumbled again into the mess.

"Damn it!" Her mother would have washed her mouth out with soap.

"Well, heya there, little one. What's a goin' on?"

A man came wobbling out of the shadows underneath the stairs that lead up to the back entrance of the Rusty Bucket saloon. "Are ya hurt?"

Annie looked around, and, when she saw no one else within earshot, all the pain in her ankle seemed inconsequential to the tightening knot of fear in her stomach. She tried again to get to her feet, leaning all her weight on her good leg. "I'm okay," she lied. Her mouth began to water as though she were about to vomit, though if it were from the pain, the stench, or fear, she could not say.

The man stumbled forward, the long shadow of his body swaying into the moonlight. His hat was pulled low, the brim casting darkness over his eyes. He approached with the unsteady movement of a drunk.

"You'n want some help there, little—"

"No. Leave me alone."

The man's shoulders snapped to attention. "There ain't no need to get all fussed. I's jus' wantin' to help ya. I gotta horse over there." He pointed a wavering finger attached to a limp wrist toward a dark area behind the alley. A place where the moon did not touch. "I could take ya home." The man's voice lowered, almost a submissive tone.

The Massacre at Yellow Hill

He moved closer, the shadow from his hat doing nothing to hide the gaze pinned to Annie.

"If you come any closer, I'll scream. Just leave me alone." She tested a little more weight on her hurt leg. A lance of pain spiked through her leg and she yelped again; it felt like someone had stuffed a burning coal into her boot.

The drunk leaped at her. His thick hands snatched her around the shoulders. "You just hush now—"

Injured ankle or no, Annie planted her weight on her good leg and fired her other foot into the man's crotch. The kick landed with a meaty thud, but pain from the impact sent her back into the wet muck, her foot caught between the man's crossed knees.

Both of them grunted in pain. The drunk man tumbled face-first into the sand beside her.

"Help!" she screamed, "H—" His hand shot out and clapped over her mouth, filling it with rancid grit. She gagged.

"Shut up," he said. And squeezed her jaw so hard her teeth grinded together. "Just calm yer ass down."

Annie swung her fists into his face. She clawed at him, buried her nails deep into his brow, and raked his eyes. She scratched and kicked and wailed with all her strength. Sucking rank air through her nostrils, trying desperately to force his hand from her face.

The world flashed white and her ears exploded with a high-pitched whine. Thick mucus and the sharp tang of blood filled her mouth. The man slapped her across the face again, turning the white to black with yellow lights around the edges of her vision.

"Can't let no girl be doin' this to me," he said. He straddled her chest, pinning her arms to her sides with his shins.

She went to holler again, but his hand was pressed so tight against her mouth that her teeth began to grind together. Her hands flailed, slapping against one of his boots, and something hard tucked inside it. Something that felt like a handle.

He had a boot knife.

"I'm gonna give you such a whoopin' and then some, girlie."

She strained against his weight, shifting her arm as low as she could manage to grip the knife handle.

She opened her eyes to see the drunk had his fist lifted high in the air, ready to crush her skull. The knife was still hooked in the boot and she couldn't pull it free. She squeezed her eyes shut in anticipation of the blow and jerked on the knife handle.

It came free of his boot, and she angled the blade upward.

Then, the sound of a butcher slapping a wet slab of beef against his block resounded in her ears. Before she could bring the knife to bear, the drunk flew off of her. Annie paid no mind to where he went as she drew in a hard, ragged breath. She hacked and coughed and spilled out her supper into the mud, the grit shredding the soft tissue inside her throat.

She turned and saw a man on top of the drunk, his right hand lifted then shot downward.

Thwack!

"Goddamn you, Earl."

Thwack!

The new stranger stood over the man he called Earl, throwing punches into the man's face until the drunk stopped trying to twist away.

Annie rolled to her knees, the knife still clutched in her hand. She began to crawl toward Earl, who now lay flat on his back. The stranger turned around.

Annie recognized him: Charlie Gathers.

He said something to her, a question of some kind, but she paid him no mind. Instead, vision hazy with rage, she stared at the drunk. The flickering light of the saloon's alley lamps revealed his face, now ravaged with deep lacerations. The bridge of his nose had collapsed, giving him the appearance of some malformed demon.

All her anger, all her fear, welled up inside her. Furious at what he'd done and terrified of what he might have done, she lifted the knife. The blade shimmered in the flickering light and Charlie went to grab her arm, but she brought the knife down quick. The steel blade drove into Earl's throat, puncturing the soft flesh as easily as carving a jack-o'-lantern.

"Ah, Christ," Charlie said as Earl's vitae spilled out of his neck and splashed all over Annie's hands and dress. He took hold of her shoulders, watching as a fountain of blood spilled out of Earl's throat. She jerked the boot knife free, and Earl's eyes shot open. He opened his mouth to scream. A gurgling whistle exited his ruptured windpipe.

Then, with a violent scream more animal than human, Annie drove the knife into one of his eyes. A meaty squish followed by a grinding crunch came from a muffled place in his skull.

Earl stopped whistling.

Stopped moving.

Stopped.

"Ah, shit. Ah, shit." Charlie ran his hands through his sweat-matted hair.

Annie looked at the dead man for a moment, then turned to Charlie. "He hurt me," she said, her voice sounding nothing like her own.

Slowly, the flat anger inside Annie began to ebb. Her lips trembled, and her shoulders rolled into a convulsing sob.

She wrapped her arms around Charlie's waist. Her fingers clenched the cloth of his shirt, balling the extra fabric in her blood-soaked hands.

Charlie's head snapped left and right, looking around furiously. "We've got to hurry."

He knelt down to the weeping child, gently pulling her away from his chest where she sobbed. Her eyes, their color that reminded him of George's eyes, just before Charlie had smashed his face with the big blacksmith hammer. He'd done it only because Hart, a malicious son of a bitch, wanted to hide the truth from everyone in Yellow Hill. Charlie hadn't acted fast enough inside the mine—he hadn't taken action to save George's life—but maybe he could save the miner's daughter. He wasn't about to fail George Miller's family. Not again.

"I knew your daddy, Annie. He was a good man, an honest man."

She looked at him with wide eyes dripping with tears.

"I'm not an honest man, Annie. I told a lot of lies to people about what happened to your daddy. And now, I'm gonna tell some more lies to the people of this town, but they're gonna be lies that'll protect you, okay?"

Still half-frozen in the foggy aftermath of her violence, she managed to nod.

"Can you walk?" he asked. "Can you run?"

Annie tested her ankle, wincing in pain. "I...I don't know."

"Well, you gotta, no matter if you think you can or not. Skin off those bloody threads and take my coat." He slipped off the long brown duster he wore. "You put this on, and you hurry through every shadow in town. Run home, and don't let no one see you. When I get back, and I get done with my lying, I'm gonna come see you and your ma. I'm gonna start telling the truth then and there, starting with your family."

She did as he said. Half-running, half-limping, Annie slipped through the night, past a search party comprised of Reverend

The Massacre at Yellow Hill

Callum, Georgie, and her mother. They called for her, crying out a name that she no longer felt was her own. The knowledge that she had changed was immediate, even if the nature or severity of the change was not. Careful as a coyote, she stuck close to the shadows as Mr. Gathers had said to, his long jacket trailing behind like a pair of wings heavy with mud. Those wings that carried her to her home, where she crawled back through the window into her room.

Annie hid the coat under her bed, then scrubbed her hands viciously in her small basin to scrape away the sticky film of blood and filth. She slipped on her nightgown and went out to the front porch. The world gleamed about her like a dream, and, in that dream, she sat in her father's old rocking chair. The chair she so often saw him sitting in when she came home from school. It was there, looking out into the darkness, that she contemplated what she had done. The thought of it made everything she looked at seem flat, unfocused, almost as if the things in the real world weren't real at all. Nothing would ever be as real as the look on Earl's face. Nothing would ever feel as real as the pressure of his throat giving way so easily to the knife. Or the blood that flowed out of the slender gap.

A while later—she didn't know how long—she awoke to her mother snatching her out of the rocking chair by the arm. Terrified, Annie braced her shoulders for a rebuke that never came.

But her mother only held her tight, scolding her over and over. "Don't you ever run off from this house ever again!" and "What would we do if something terrible happened to you?"

Something terrible had happened, though.

Terrible things were always happening, it seemed. Annie had lost her father, and now she'd lost herself.

She clutched her mother, only saying she was sorry over and over.

Tabitha tried to console her, but Annie despaired under the full moon. She embraced her mother tighter, trying to hold on to anything that felt familiar.

Chapter Nineteen

YELLOW HILL, TEXAS

CHARLIE THREW EARL'S body over his horse, then waited until the streets were empty. He rode three miles outside of town to a dense mesquite thicket.

As he dug, morning came. The crown of the sun rose, driving away the night sky and stars, transforming the black to purple and gold and pink. Under all that morning color, Charlie used his pickax to break the ground, but it took a tin dinner plate to clear the sand, lime and caliche from the hole. When his hands began to hurt, he dug a bit more but stopped soon thereafter.

Burning the body would have been best, but he couldn't risk waking eyes seeing the smoke.

Charlie gripped Earl by the ankles and pulled him into the hole. He tried not to look at the knife hilt pointing back at him like an accusation from the eye socket.

You did this to me, the corpse proclaimed in silence. *You beat me senseless and then let a little girl murder me. Charlie Gathers, you are a cowardly son of a bitch.*

Charlie didn't know if he was a coward. Rather than hope that he wasn't, he told himself this would be the last dead body he would ever have to mutilate, hide, or lie about.

He was so far from Virginia, so far from home. So far from where he thought he was going to be five years ago. Texas was supposed to be the place where he made his fortune, not the place where cruel fortune placed him.

Lucas had known what Charlie now knew. The thing that Earl Thomas would now never see: Yellow Hill was a place with enough wealth to sustain a thousand generous men, but only a single greedy one. Jeremiah Hart's tyranny over the town was absolute, and, under his dominion, the town would always suffer.

If Charlie stayed, he'd die as either an elderly pauper or a middling foreman. Hart had beaten on him, blamed him for Micah's death because they had been arguing in the tent while young Micah had tried to play one-man-army inside the mine.

Charlie decided to leave, and right quick, but his conscience wouldn't let him ride out of town before he made things right with the widow Miller and her children. What was left of his pride wouldn't let him leave without confronting his son-of-a-bitch employer either. That piece of his dignity, he told himself, was something he'd be taking with him when he saddled his horse and headed to any place greener than this. Charlie would be the final link in a chain of Gathers working under millionaire prospector Jeremiah Hart.

Sweaty from a half-day's work done in the course of a couple of hours, Charlie covered the mound of dirt over Earl's body with enough mesquite brambles to ensure no one would think to walk there.

As he saddled his horse to head back to town, he came to the epiphany that the desert wasn't for him; it wasn't his country. It hid too many secrets and was home to too many monsters, both human and ungodly.

Chapter Twenty

YELLOW HILL, TEXAS

JEREMIAH WAS IN his rose garden when Charlie Gathers came riding up from the south side of town. He was a long way off, riding toward the main drag of Yellow Hill, when Jeremiah said, "Why the hell isn't he at the mine?"

No one was around to hear him. The house was empty of all life. His own life was now a prison of obsessive reading and secret ritual.

His daytime existence was still in order. Mornings were for managing his ledger, and afternoons were spent in his vaulted study pouring over the manuscript, only to break at four to send a daily wire to Chicago: a progress update to his benefactors. The miners had found the antechamber, and now Jeremiah was close—oh, so close—to deciphering the full ritual that would make him the key to a gate. It would be one of the lesser gates, but a gate nonetheless.

But nights in the Hart House were not the same since Micah's death. Though he often retired by nine, Jeremiah found himself more regularly snapping awake at the desk in his shadow-filled study, where the oil lamps hung from their hooks, exhausted. The manuscript would be open, a pen in his hand, the ink still shimmering wet where a fresh line of translation lay scrawled across his notebook.

Micah, his sweet son, had been his only tether to the regularity of sane hours. Some nights, he would sit by Jeremiah's bedroom door after he went to sleep, in case his father rose , as he did on occasion, and walked toward the study in his sleep. Always in his sleep, always toward the study.

Toward the manuscript.

Micah would see his father step out of his room in only his nightclothes, take him by the hand, and guide him away from the lamp-lighted study and back to bed. But there were some nights that the manuscript—yes, it had to be the manuscript drawing him awake each night—pulled his will harder than his son could overcome with his gentle care.

Now, without Micah, Jeremiah rarely slept. Only thirty minutes on his pocket watch passed between when he remembered sleeping and when he awoke to find himself leaning over his desk, pen scribbling across the page.

The red letters on the black manuscript burned images and words and illumination of some great purpose into his mind. It was guiding him, leading him to some kind of keystone or phrase. Perhaps an incantation that would deliver unto him the great power that slept inside the mine. The monstrous sentinels that had ravaged his son could not be bypassed until he knew the words to command them. When that moment came, he would go into that dark cavern and emerge from it with a power total in its sum and revelatory in its effect.

The Society of Prometheus wanted it for themselves, naturally. For the High Priest. But Jeremiah was the one who had risked all his wealth and sacrificed a wife and now his only heir to the mission of garnering a power that could set the world right, a world that had become a human wasteland. A world that had forgotten the old ways. The forgotten ways. 'And what man had forgotten,' Lucio Gandolfi had written, 'the Nine remember.'

The High Priest of the Society had the power and Gandolfi had his masterful research, but it would be Jeremiah Hart who would find the method of the Nine's return. He would find the wheel of the world, and when he did, it would be Jeremiah Hart who captained the turn. No one else had given so much to the cause. Not the High Priest's Baroness. Not Lady Tanzer or Captain Barron. None of them had known sacrifice such as this. Not even Grey, who had lost his life in bleeding Kansas to protect the very copy of the manuscript that Jeremiah now pored over each night.

Grey was luckiest of them all to have died so young. It was happier for a man to die for a cause rather than to sacrifice everything that had made life worth living. Grey, that skeleton of a man, had no wife. He had never held a son whose birthright would have made him the first benefactor of a freshly renewed world.

Jeremiah's grief flooded his heart, making it too great to bear. The lower his grief sank, the higher the flame of his anger rose. That anger, alloyed with his singular occult purpose, centered him. Drove him. Whipped away his overwhelming fatigue. Dominated him.

And so, there in his rose garden, Jeremiah snipped yellow roses from their stalks and gently laid them into a wicker basket. Susan, his late wife, had woven it only a few months before Micah was born, and he thought it the perfect vessel to carry the flowers to the cemetery. He would speak quietly, lay the roses upon the two plots, and tell them how deeply he wished they could have been here for his moment of triumph. To those ghosts, he would tell all the truth.

After that, he would lie. He would wire his regular report of progress to the society members, telling them that months of work were still required to follow the emerald vein of stone leading to the ancient place of worship. The hidden vestibule in the cave had taken years of his life and a fortune to find, costing him everything. Months, he would tell them, though he was sure the translation and ritual would be complete in a day, maybe two. Three at the most.

The time was near. He was so close.

Close enough to send off his final earthly farewells.

Chapter Twenty-One

THE PERMIAN BASIN

ON THE ROAD to Yellow Hill, the sun lorded over Carson and Ptolemy like a wrathful god. A rare breeze swirled over the duo, but it fluttered away even quicker than it had come.

Carson looked upon endless hills of sun-bleached sand rolling out forever. Abraham was lathered in sweat, his head bobbing up and down as they trekked further along the blistering path exiting the Llano Estacado. The gnarled limbs of mesquite were the only signs of life. Carson hadn't seen flower or fowl in the last day and a half of riding.

Sweat rolled off Ptolemy's chin in large drops, but he rode on without complaint. They hadn't spoken much since they left Big Spring. Ptolemy wasn't a man to speak his way through the challenges before him; he was more of an intellectual hermit. Carson had learned very quickly that when his father was ready to speak, he would.

The boy tried to learn from example but found it hard to keep his concentration from drifting away from the problems and ghosts that haunted him: the Society of Prometheus, the vampire knight Sigurd, his own tumble down the flight of stairs, the visions of Shirley's face when he gunned her down. They came to him in his daydreams, and they made him shiver while baking in the hard sun.

Would his world always be filled with such terrifying visions? More importantly, why did God allow these things to exist?

"Pa," Carson said, daring to break his father's concentration. "Why does God allow so much bad in the world?"

Ptolemy pulled Vanilla to a stop and sighed. He looked over at his boy. "There comes a time when every person asks that question, son, and ultimately there are two answers. I think you're already figuring on the first one."

"There ain't no real God," Carson said.

Ptolemy nodded. "Ezra made that determination near his end. The more he went through that damnable manuscript, the more he jabbered on and on about a darker kind of cosmology. The God of the Bible, he thought, was a myth folks made up to make themselves feel better, but that there were other gods out there. And he did not believe them to be kind."

Carson squinted against the bright light of the sun. "What's the other choice?"

"That God is real, and that He's the origin of love in the world. And it is that love that cuts through the evil that exists inside the hearts of men and all other creatures. Those who follow him are called to root out injustice and slay evil. Love ferociously."

"What do you think, Pa?"

"I think it's a little bit of the former and mostly the latter. I see both in the world. With the life you've lived, much of it has been a passage through the dark places most people never see, but don't let that steal hope away from you, son. A life without hope ain't no way of livin'. Every man, in his own time, decides which way he's goin' to think. You will too."

Ptolemy nodded at the boy, then gave Vanilla a little kick.

As they rode on, Carson went back to daydreaming, where he was visited again by his familiar monstrosities.

They didn't speak again for a long while.

Chapter Twenty-Two

YELLOW HILL, TEXAS

———————

THE HEAT OF the day refused to break as Charlie Gathers stood hat in hand at the doorstep of the Miller home, nervously thumbing the brim of his hat with grimy fingers. He knocked.

"Who is it?" the widow Miller said from inside.

"It's Charlie Gathers, ma'am. I was hoping I might have a word with you and your family on an account of George."

He heard some murmurings behind the door and then silence.

After a few moments, the widow responded. "It was a hard night for us, Mr. Gathers, and I believe I've heard all I want to hear from you about George. Please leave."

Charlie shook his head. "Afraid I can't do that. I lied to you before, Mrs. Miller. I lied to you about what happened that night in the mine. About what happened to your husband. I've come to give you the truth."

The bolt on the door unlatched, and he sighed deeply. The door opened. Charlie never thought that Tabitha was overly pretty, but there was something about how the morning light touched her skin and bright blue eyes that he found honest and appealing.

"What lies, Charlie?" she asked, her voice calm. Quiet. And with a gesture of her chin, she invited him inside.

Annie and the boy were there too. All four of them sat in the front parlor. It was there that Charlie told them the story of the creature in the mine, and of how George had really died, and how Jeremiah Hart had demanded that he tell the lies.

Tabitha sat across from Charlie, her posture perfect and her mouth agape.

He didn't want to tell them about what they'd done with the hammers, but when Tabitha asked why George's body had appeared crushed, he was forced to confess the truth.

Georgie sat beside his mother, his eyes glazed over, almost as if he were incapable of fully understanding.

Annie kept her head low, never meeting his eyes.

"That's why you have to leave, Mrs. Miller. You have to take your children, and you have to run away from this godforsaken place. The miners found some kind of cave behind a wall of limestone, and whatever is living in that place killed Mr. Marple, Micah Hart, and another older miner who was dumb enough to go in with him. I'm telling you all of these terrible things because you deserve to know. All of you deserve to know the truth."

Tabitha shook her head, and when her chin lifted, tears fell down her cheeks. "How dare you come into this house and spread this kind of vicious...joke?"

"It ain't no tomfoolery. It ain't no vicious—"

"You son of a bitch." She stood up and glared at him.

The words hit Charlie like a punch in the gut.

"Mrs. Miller, please, I swear to God, Christ, and all his angels that I am telling you the truth. You have to get your children—"

"Is this how Mr. Hart expects to run us out of town? Putting one of his dogs to feed me this story, forcing us to relive the pain of losing my husband?" She swept a hand through the air, tracing over Annie and Georgie. "Their father?"

"I ain't his man anymore," said Charlie, his voice low. "I'm going to confront him, quit my post, and leave town before nightfall. The truth of it is, I'm terrified, ma'am. I'm scared to death that Hart is going to send me back into that mine. I won't have it, and I won't work for him another second. But my conscience wouldn't let me leave without bearing the truth of it all."

Tabitha's eyes narrowed. "You are a particular kind of bastard." She stood up without further word and walked to her bedroom.

He knew something was wrong when he looked and saw both children gawking wide-eyed to the open door of her bedroom.

"You have to believe me," he called, pleading. "I swear I wouldn't— Ah, shit!"

Tabitha came striding out of her bedroom, a shotgun cradled against her shoulder.

Georgie and Annie cried out.

Charlie faced his palms at her, leaning back against the chair, away from the gun. "Mrs. Miller, please—"

"Get out of my house, Charlie, or I swear to God I'll kill you in front of my own children." She aimed the barrel at the foreman's face.

"Momma, stop!" Annie screamed. "Stop it right now!"

Georgie wailed.

"Mrs—"

"No! Not another word, Charlie Gathers. My family has lost everything. We are abused by poverty, and we have taken more than our fair share of tragedy from this town."

"Momma, please." Annie said, her voice shrill. "You can't!"

"And why can't I? You don't understand. You don't know all the misfortune this man and his employer have wrought on our family."

Annie screamed at her mother. "Because last night, when I ran off, a man attacked me behind the saloon and was gonna hurt me. I didn't get my bruises from a fall. And…"

Tabitha's shoulders shrunk as she dared to take her eyes off Charlie. "And what, honey?"

Annie began to cry. "The man attacked me, and I killed him, Momma. And Mr. Gathers saved my life."

Chapter Twenty-Three

THE PERMIAN BASIN

———

CHOPPING THROUGH THE sand at full gallop, Carson didn't hear himself screaming. It was a full-throated blast deafened only by the thundering hooves of Abraham and Vanilla.

The bandits had come upon them on the road and were gaining on the father and son. They were so close that Ptolemy had jerked his revolver from his holster, turned his shoulders high in the saddle, and fired at the four men giving chase on horseback.

Four times Ptolemy fired.

Four times he missed.

"Kick for the thicket!" Ptolemy hollered, holding the revolver's smoking barrel toward the sky.

Carson squeezed hard into the gelding. A raw power unloosed in the animal as it quickened its gait, sending the two of them bursting past the older mare. The boy's weight was nothing to Abraham, light as a bag of goose feathers.

Muscles rippling in the arid bone-white sunlight, Abraham carried Carson so swiftly, the boy thought he might leave the whole world behind. Carson posted high in the saddle, leaning forward, cutting into the sandy wind.

A volley of lead screamed past him, exploding mesquite and fruitless mulberry branches into the air like parade confetti.

With the last rush of adrenaline spent from Abraham, Carson felt the horse begin to lag. He was tiring, heavily lathered. Sooner or later, Carson and Ptolemy were going to have to turn and fight.

The boy had killed monsters before, though never a man, and everything was happening so fast that it wasn't until his gelding had carried him into a crop of trees that his trepidation set in.

Vanilla came chuffing into the small wood behind him. Ptolemy's eyes were wide, not with fear but with rage.

"Grab your rifle and get down," he ordered.

Carson obeyed. The sheriff's thirty-thirty slid cleanly from the well-oiled sheath. Without hesitation, Carson cranked the leaver action and leveled the barrel at the bandits.

Ptolemy slapped a hand around the barrel and jerked the rifle from the boy's hand, as if conflicting his previous command. "No."

"But—"

"Don't argue, son. Take the horses further back into the brush, in between the trees, and keep them safe."

A thick limb of gnarled mesquite exploded just beside Carson, and he screamed.

"Go, damn it!" Ptolemy turned back and fired.

"No!" Carson's voice broke high and tinny like a snapping piano wire. "Damn you if you think we're splitting up again." He turned, loosed a thick branch of mesquite from a tree, and cropped both horses on the rear. "Get!"

First Vanilla, then Abraham, went galloping through the thicket and vanished out the other side.

The Massacre at Yellow Hill

Ptolemy flared a look at him that almost broke his spirit, then he pushed them both down into the sand as bullets whizzed over their heads.

The echo of the bandit's guns died among the desert sands. Over the ringing in his ears, Carson could hear the men whooping and laughing threats in Spanish.

Ptolemy slid his saddlebag across the ground at Carson, drew his revolver, and tossed it to the boy. "Your sawed-off is no good this far away. Reload the revolver and hand it back to me when my rifle is spent."

Carson nodded, broke the cylinder out of the revolver, and, with trembling hands, poured the hot casings from their housing. One caught him on the wrist, burning him, but he bit down and reached for fresh ammunition.

Ptolemy wrenched his body around, set his elbow deep into the ground, and then cursed, aimed, and fired.

Carson looked up just in time to see a bandit's head snap back where the bullet caught him in the forehead. The man went limp, sitting straight up in the saddle, then tipped to one side. A puff of sandy powder blasted into the air when the man's face slapped into the ground.

Boom. The rifle roared. Click-clack.

Boom. Click-clack.

A steady rhythm of gunfire from Ptolemy saw another bandit take a bullet in the chest, sending him flipping off the back of a painted mustang.

The bandits were on them now, not twenty feet away, when a bullet slapped the sand in front of Carson, sending grit into his eyes.

"Revolver!" Ptolemy cried.

Blind and terrified, Carson tossed the revolver toward his father's voice.

He rubbed at his eyes, feeling the grit tearing at his eyeballs. Gunfire boomed all around him. Vision still blurry, he pulled his sawed-off twenty-gauge from his hip and cocked both hammers back.

Something big and heavy stomped the ground in front of the boy then landed behind him. No doubt, one of the bandits had unknowingly ridden right over the top of him, missing him by less than a foot.

Carson spun on his back, pointed the wide barrels blindly, and let loose with heavy shot. A horse shrieked and a man cried out.

Ptolemy's revolver oppressed the air again. A man cursed in Spanish, then went silent.

Carson rubbed at his face with the sleeve of his shirt.

An unfamiliar voice bellowed, "No, no queirdo Dios! No! Por favor, ayúdame."

"Estas armado," hollered Ptolemy.

"No," the bandit weakly. Almost a mumble.

Ptolemy hooked his strong hands around Carson's shoulders and hoisted the boy to his feet. He dusted the boy's clothes as he searched for signs of injury, his fingers fumbling with worry. "Are you hit?"

"I don't...I don't think so," Carson said with little confidence. "What did he say?"

"He's dying. Asking God for help," said Ptolemy

He continued to search the boy for wounds, his fingers slipping through his son's sweat-soaked hair. Satisfied, he walked over to the last living bandit, his revolver dangling heavy in his dark hand.

"Aye, por dios mio," the man said.

The bandit lay in the dirt clutching his stomach, his fingers slick with dark blood. Ptolemy pointed the revolver at the dying man, then dared to look away and scan the horizon all around them.

The Massacre at Yellow Hill

"What are we going to do with him, Pa?" Carson said.

"Speak English," Ptolemy said to the man. "How many more of you are there?"

Writhing in pain, the man managed to answer by shaking his head.

"Por favor," he said, his voice trembling. "Por favor Dios."

Carson looked at the bandit, the man's eyes were drawn open so wide. Every limb trembling.

"He's been shot through the stomach," said Ptolemy. "Even if we were close to a town with a doctor, he wouldn't make it."

"We can't leave him here to die."

"You're right." Ptolemy pulled the hammer back on his revolver. "Look away, son."

"What? No!"

The air split with thunder, and the cap of the bandit's head blow open like a shattered piece of pottery, coating the sand in bloody gray chunks.

Ptolemy's head was low, a grim countenance on his face, as the echo from the revolver melted to silence.

Carson exploded into rage. Rushing over to his adopted father, he threw a balled fist into his chest. The thudding impact stung his hand. "No, no!" the boy wailed and waylaid Ptolemy to impotent effect.

Ptolemy clutched the boy tightly to his chest. He ended the embrace abruptly, knelt in front of Carson, and took him by the shoulders. "Listen to me, son. Listen to me."

"No!"

"Listen—"

"You killed him. You shot a helpless man."

"I shot him as a mercy, son. If I hadn't, he would have died slowly, painfully, over hours. If we tried to take him with us, we'd be carrying a blood trail for all manner of beasts to fall upon us in the night. Coyotes, wolves, crows…and those are just the things we know are looking for prey out in his desert."

Carson broke into wild sobs. His shoulders shook violently, and his heart ached. "We could have saved him!"

"That man," Ptolemy began, the words a curse, "along with all his companions, came upon us as murderers and thieves. What if they had killed me, Carson? What if they'd killed you? Then one of us would be alone in this world. All alone…again. Whoever he was, he made a choice to murder and steal as his occupation, and so long as I am alive, I'll never allow someone to take you from me."

The wind slashed through the air, swirling sand all about their squinting wet faces.

"I love you that much, son. I love you enough to do terrible things to man or creature that would try to harm you. My care will not abide it."

Carson shook his head. His lips were still trembling.

"I know it's hard, but you have to choke it down for now. We have to find our horses, or our situation will be dire."

The boy found his hat underneath one of the bandits that Ptolemy had shot. When he saw that it was soaked through with blood, he left it behind and went to look for Abraham among the thicket.

It took only an hour to find their horses, but the sun pounded relentlessly on them the whole time. Exhausted, Carson found that his hands shook and his mind was foggy. He brushed over Abraham for injury, but found that, almost miraculously, the horse had made it out of the fight mostly unscathed. Vanilla, on the other hand, had a bright red gash running across the white patch on her yellow face. One liquid brown eye blinked furiously, swatting away the drops of blood blurring her vision.

The Massacre at Yellow Hill

Ptolemy gave the horses the last two apples in his satchel, which they chomped greedily. Father and son walked side by side, guiding the chuffing horses by their reins through the withering desert landscape. Not long before night fell, they found a stagnant pond just off the trail. They made camp there, building a fire from mesquite trees, where they rinsed the sand from their mouths and chewed on hard biscuits and salted beef. The horses sloshed to the center of the water, where they drank heavily and chewed wildflowers and spindles of grass that had sprouted near the pond's edge.

Ptolemy said that he would take the first watch. He sat across from the boy, smoking his pipe as he stared into the flicking tongues of the flame.

When the silver moon hung at a quarter of its height within a forever-reaching sky, Carson spoke for the first time since the fight. "I don't want to do this anymore," he said.

"Do what, son?"

"I don't want to hurt people anymore."

Ptolemy blew a long line of smoke from his lips, saying nothing.

"I don't like killing," Carson said. "I hate the way it makes me feel. Doesn't matter if it's vampires or regular folk, I hate it. I don't think I wanna do this...all of this anymore."

"There is no doubt that killin' steals a piece from a man every time he does it. Honestly, I'd be more worried if you said you enjoyed it, and I'm glad to hear that you don't..."

"But—"

"But there are things in this world, both human and inhuman, that require men of their time to take action. Bible says that as a man's wisdom increases, so does his sorrow. That's right, I think. This is the sorrow you carry. I carry it too, along with all the rest of the weights of life. Even if you quit now, son, even if you turn your

187

back on this mission of ours, it won't stop what's coming. If Lucas Ramos was right, if the Society of Prometheus has its way, it'll see all the world ravaged by creatures far worse than those bandits and that vampire in Big Spring. You've read from the black manuscript; you know what they are apt to do. What they're wont to unleash."

"I don't care," said Carson. "I don't want to feel this way."

Ptolemy nodded, the sweet smoke from his pipe swirling around his dark face. "That's apathy, and apathy is the death of hope. Trust me when I say, Carson, that a life without hope is like a ship without an anchor. Apathy is a rot that grows in the faint-hearted. Only a man with great courage can carry hope. And I don't think you're a coward. I've seen your bravery too many times."

The words fell heavily on Carson. After what had happened with Ezra, who had tried to sacrifice his own son to bring about what he called 'the Shifting of the Stars,' he and Ptolemy had made vows to one another that they would work to end the Society of Prometheus and cure the world of the dark registry of monsters that sought to prey on the weak. He'd made those vows when the fires of betrayal were still fresh in his heart. It was only now that he wished he had never promised Ptolemy anything but his love.

"Why does it have to be us, Pa? Why can't someone else do it?"

"Being chosen to a purpose such as ours is a calling that feels more like a curse. Make no mistake, we are chosen for this purpose; and no matter where it takes us, we cannot falter. Else we all stand to lose."

"Lose what?" asked the boy.

"Everything, son. We stand to lose each other and the world along with it."

Chapter Twenty-Four

YELLOW HILL, TEXAS

CHARLIE GATHERS STOOD on the widow's porch, staring up at Hart's three-story home in the distance. His cigarette smoldered between his lips, the rising smoke curled in the windless afternoon. The widow sat nearby in a wicker chair, watching him. She had gone to put the children to bed not long before, and when she came back, she told him this had been the second most difficult day of her life. Her family had lost and lost and lost with no sign of reprieve.

"There seems to be very little in the way of justice in this part of the world," the widow said, "or in this part of my life."

Charlie didn't know much about justice, so he said the only thing he could think to say. "I buried the body far outside of town."

Tabitha remained silent, only nodding.

"Earl didn't have no kin, and he was pretty squirrely anyhow. Folks will guess he just left. Several other men have left since what happened to George and the others. Won't matter if they find him anyway. No way anyone would suspect your daughter."

Tabitha sat there quietly, rocking back and forth.

"My hope is that you won't worry about that," he said.

"I'm not worried about people finding the body, Mr. Gathers. I'm worried about my little girl. What happened to her," said Tabitha, her eyes clear and bright in the afternoon sun. "What she did. I'm feel ashamed—"

"She killed in self-defense, ma'am, I don't reckon you should feel ashamed of her."

"Yes. In self-defense," said Tabitha. "And you misunderstand me. I'm not ashamed of my daughter for killing Earl Thomas; I'm ashamed that my daughter lives in a world that required her to do it."

A portion of Charlie felt wounded at that, though he was sure the remark wasn't directly aimed at him. Still, it struck him. "Again, I am sorry for my lies. For what happened to your husband. Please know I am deeply ashamed of them myself."

At the statement, the widow turned away. "You mean to leave tonight then?" Her voice was distant.

"I do," said Charlie, turning his eyes back toward the Hart home. "Right after I head up to that house and tell that son of a bitch that I'm done. Members of my family have worked for him since the time he formed his company in Chicago. My father and my uncle, both of them lived, worked, and died under his employ. I will not let him use me up in the same fashion."

"Where will you go?" asked the widow.

"Probably back up north somewhere. Got an old friend who works up in Colorado. Big coal boom going on up there in a place called Black Wells. Won't be a foreman anymore, but I never liked being the boss in the first place. I'm good at busting stone, that's no doubt, but being responsible for other men…just never felt like my place."

The Massacre at Yellow Hill

"After George died, I considered heading to Colorado myself. I have a sister who lives in Denver. Married a gambler. We haven't seen or written each other in years. In truth, Mr. Gathers, I don't know where we'll go or how we'll get there." She grunted a laugh, half-disgusted. "And here I was thinking that I'd take up George's pick and go working in the mine myself. What a joke that was."

Charlie turned and looked at the widow. Her face was harder than it ought to have been, the plainness of her features magnified to something close to pretty by the bright fury of her eyes. The skin was weathered, creased by years she had not yet lived, bearing the seams of time and worry that had stolen almost all the softness of her youth.

"Honestly, Mrs. Miller…" He took a long drag off his cigarette. "If I had the money, I'd give it to you and your children here and now. But I wasted it all on cards, women, and whiskey. I wish I could take it all back, if it would just allow me to give you that kindness you and your children deserve."

She didn't return his gaze. "I appreciate what you did for Annie, but pardon me if I've grown tired of conversing about all the things men either promised or wished they had done for me. George promised that we'd strike it rich out here. Make our fortune. When that didn't happen, he'd spend nights telling me that we'd try another plot when he saved up enough money from mining. Even then, I knew he was just voicing his regret. Dreams don't come true out here, Mr. Gathers. God and Jeremiah Hart have seen to that."

Charlie's head dropped in consideration. "Well, I aim to rectify that for myself now. I hope that chance comes for you and yours too."

The widow looked over to him. And with the red sunset burning behind her, she dismissed him. "Go on, Mr. Gathers. Go do what you need to do. And go knowing that whatever little forgiveness I have left in me, I give it to you."

"I am truly sorry," he said, his bottom lip trembling around the words.

"For what it's worth," she said, "so am I."

He stepped off the porch and went over to his horse. He pulled himself up in a single smooth motion. Part of him, though he did not know why, hoped that the widow would be watching him depart. In his heart, he wanted very badly for the two of them to lock eyes, even if for one last time, hoping that whatever might have been or whatever might become noble within Charlie Gathers, the widow would see in the red evening.

But Tabitha Miller was not watching him. She only sat upon the porch watching the dunes as the falling sun, for a time, turned the pale sand to gold. The slice of sunlight, lasting only a few heartbeats, caught the rim of the world and the woman, glorifying them both.

Charlie trotted though town, his horse heavily laden with all the worldly possessions he cared to take. He'd made a mistake with the way he'd lied about George's death, but he felt somehow vindicated by what he'd done for the daughter. It was enough to let him move forward with his life, out of the employment of Hart, out of the post of foreman, and most important to him, out of the goddamn wasteland of the West Texas desert. Pretty sunsets be damned; he missed the tall, dark mountains up north, ached for the snow and the winding rivers that cut through the Smoky Mountains. Charlie's home. The place he had been born. He belonged in wet green places, not the vast mesquite-choked sands where he'd buried Earl, and those green places were where he was going, right after he gave Jeremiah Hart a piece of his mind. And if the old, rich bastard wasn't careful with his words, Charlie would deliver a beating such as only the strong hands of a miner could provide.

The three-story ranch house stood tall against the rolling dunes of the dark horizon. The exterior of the home was pitch black, save for a single light that flickered from a second-story window. Hart's study light. The thought of whipping his employer's ass among his vault of books suited Charlie just fine. He'd been in fistfights since he was a boy, became an accomplished knife fighter before twenty, and he'd only seen Hart wear a revolver twice, never once firing it.

Charlie couldn't believe that he'd ever allowed himself to be scared of Jeremiah Hart. He was almost a head taller than Charlie, but he carried little weight and showed no scars from learning how to tussle.

The miner almost hoped that Hart said the wrong thing. Ran that thin, mean mouth of his. And so, sitting on his horse, just outside the house, Charlie ran the conversation over and over in his mind. Rehearsing what he'd say and just how he'd say it.

You've been a bastard to my whole family, he said, silently moving his lips with his thoughts. *I'm leaving, you son of a bitch, and there ain't nothing you or your money can do about it.*

Hart's response, Charlie weighed, would either grant him the opportunity to part ways like gentlemen or be the final provocation required to put the boots to the rich pecker-head.

He dismounted his horse and, smiling venomously, climbed the porch steps. Why give Hart the opportunity to greet him at the door? He tested the front doorknob without knocking.

It clicked open.

Of course, Charlie thought, you're not the kind of man to worry about locking your doors at night. Everyone is afraid of you, right, Jeremiah? Well, not this man. Not anymore.

The foyer, which had for so many years astonished Charlie with its lavish holdings and polished wooden floors, looked dull and unimpressive under the veil of darkness.

His smile widened when he saw the leather gun belt hanging on the knob of the banister. Hart's revolver was there, resting in the holster. As he walked past it, Charlie hocked a snotty wad on the belt. He ascended the stairs, making sure to pound his feet loudly.

"Jeremiah," he called out with all the menace within himself. "You and I got business to attend."

His fists were already clenched, his mind sharply set on the violence he might do. He wouldn't kill him, for sure, but he'd pay Hart back for the giant welt he put on Charlie's face after blaming him for Micah's death.

He called out again, but the only reply was silence. The heavy iron door that served as the barrier to Hart's study was pulled almost shut. The second story was all shadow except for a thick strip of wavering yellow that ran like a slash along the door frame of the study.

Charlie took the heavy brass handle in his hand and pulled the door open.

Chapter Twenty-Five

YELLOW HILL, TEXAS

WHILE HER CHILDREN slept, Tabitha Miller considered fate and time, dark monsters, and the sham of providence. Though Charlie had left over an hour ago, she found herself still sitting in George's favorite wicker chair, rising only once to wrap herself in one of her husband's old work shirts she hadn't had the strength to wash.

The smell of him had faded, but she could still breathe in the odor of pipe tobacco, sweat, and hard earth. The temperature dipped. A cool desert wind blew down through the mesquites on from the rolling dune tops. The chill of the growing night was repelled by the familiar scent and memory of the only man she had ever loved.

She turned her head when she heard the soft clopping of hooves approaching from the north end of the main thoroughfare. The moon and stars revealed themselves in a cloudless sky, and in their pale light she spied two riders. One, a tall man wreathed in shadow, guided the second horse by its reins. Behind him, a much smaller rider bobbed asleep in the saddle.

When the lead rider came close, Tabitha saw that he was a tall Black man with hard eyes.

"Evening, ma'am," he said, his voice was deep, like someone calling from the bottom of a well. When he spoke, his large teeth shone white as a freshly painted fence.

"Evening."

He brought their horses into the yellow glow of the porch lamps, and Tabitha saw that the second rider was a little boy around Annie's age with skin pale as milk.

"My name is Gilbert Ptolemy. Don't mean to be a bother, and I'm sure I know the answer, but I'd rather not arouse the anger of folks in the town if I'm correct…I was wondering if your local hotel is temperamental toward folks like me renting a room for the night? We've been riding real hard from Big Spring, and I believe a proper bed would do the boy some good."

Tabitha studied the boy who, even though they'd come to a full stop, was deep in sleep. Both their horses were lathered heavily in sweat, and the man's mare chuffed and stamped, protesting another step.

"Oscar Potter owns the hotel in town, but seeing as he fought on the losing side of the Slavers' Revolt, I don't reckon you'd be welcome, Mr. Ptolemy." She stood up and approached him without hesitation, extending her hand. "I'm Tabitha Miller."

His eyes widened as they shook hands. "Pardon me asking, ma'am, but I don't suppose you're George Miller's widow, are ya?"

Her face bent in confusion. "I am. Did you know George?"

He let her hand go, sliding his own back to his saddle horn. "No, ma'am, can't say that I did. Learned of him from a former miner here named Lucas Ramos. He told me of your late husband's fate. My condolences for your loss."

196

The Massacre at Yellow Hill

Tabitha could tell the man was being careful with his words. "And just what did Mr. Ramos tell you about my husband?" She was careful too.

"The truth, I believe. The kind of truth that folks don't often talk about outside." Vanilla chuffed and stamped again, frustrated. "Easy, Vanilla," he said. "Ma'am, I know this is forward, but if you have an extra space in your home, I'd be awfully appreciative if you'd let us borrow it for a night. I'm willing to pay you twice whatever Mr. Potter charges. And I'm willing to surrender our weapons to you, as a measure of our good faith."

She looked at the boy again, then she studied Ptolemy. "Mr. Ptolemy, but too much has befallen our family to allow a strange man to sleep in this house. Nothing to do with skin color, but seeing as I don't know you, I won't risk it. However, we do need the money, so the boy can sleep in my bed, and you can sleep out back in my husband's shed. I'd offer you more, but that's all I can afford on account of my children's safety. I'll take your guns and get the two of you settled. I don't sleep much, and if I catch you trying to make your way into the house, I'll shoot you where you stand."

Ptolemy nodded. "More than fair."

He took his revolver from the holster and handed it over to her. She took it in one hand, and with the other, she cocked the hammer back and held it at her side.

"Rifles on the porch. I'll collect them once you're both bedded down. We've got a water pump and trough by the shed. You can unburden your horses there. Don't have any straw, seeing as we haven't had a horse in years, but what grass we have, your animals are more than welcome to."

Ptolemy did as she said, moving slowly as he removed their guns and set them against the post of the porch. He took the boy by the arm, slid him off the saddle, and cradled him as if he weighed nothing.

"Come on, son," he said.

The boy mumbled but never stirred.

"He's got a squirrel gun in his belt," the man said. "You'll want to take that too."

Tabitha slid it out of the boy's holster with her other hand.

She let the man go inside first, keeping herself a few paces behind him the whole time, and directed him to her room, where he set the boy down on her bed. Standing in the hall, she let him come back through the house to exit.

Outside, she watched as he led the two horses to the shed and loosened their rigging near the trough. "Bucket?" he asked.

"By the pump," she said.

He said nothing, moving slowly as he filled the bucket many times over, pouring the water into the dusty trough. The horses took to it quickly, dipping their faces so deep that their noses disappeared beneath the dark water.

"Reckon you're gonna lock the shed once I'm inside," he said.

"Come first light, I'll let you out. Breakfast won't be much, but if you stay honest, you're both welcome to it."

"I have some questions for you tomorrow, Mrs. Miller. Questions about what happened to your husband."

"Figured you might, Mr. Ptolemy." She paused for a moment, the two of them facing each other under the light of the blue moon. "Don't betray my hospitality. I'd hate to make the boy an orphan."

After she let him use the water closet, he unsaddled the horses and followed her to the shed, carrying his saddle and sleeping roll.

"Goodnight, Mr. Ptolemy," she said.

"Goodnight, ma'am."

The Massacre at Yellow Hill

She closed the door, looped the iron padlock in the lock, and snapped it shut.

Back inside the house, she went into her room and looked at the sleeping boy. He was tall for his age, thin as a reed. His hairline was crusted with flecks of blood, and his fingers twitched as he dreamed.

Tabitha took a few extra blankets from a chest at the end of the bed and made a pallet on the living room floor so as to face the front door. If Georgie woke in the night to go to her room, she'd coax him to lay with her in the living space. She left the revolver hammer cocked, put her back against the wall, and wrestled with her tired eyes until sleep took her.

Tabitha slept deeply, waking after she found herself having strange dreams of being trapped inside a crumbling house with shadowy figures hoisting glimmering revolvers into a blood red sky. Her eyes flashed open, and she groped for the gun next to her.

It was still there.

She rose, stretching her back in the cool, dark living room while looking through the kitchen window at the shed. The dawn was just about to break. A rustling in the twilight revealed the graceful silhouettes of the horses back at the trough, lapping up whatever water remained. They were beautiful, she thought, and wondered if a horse and wagon would be all it took to get her family out of Yellow Hill. Even with what Mr. Ptolemy said he would pay, she wouldn't have near enough to afford such a luxury. A horse went for twenty-five dollars and a wagon for seventy-five.

Never had so little an amount seemed like so much.

The rent on the house was seven dollars, and she didn't even have the means to pay that at the top of the month. Even if she sold all their furniture and her mother's china and George's shotgun, she'd still only have enough for a single horse. Disgusted with her circumstances, she put the thought of money out of her mind and walked down the hall.

Tabitha checked on her children first. She found Georgie sleeping in bed with Annie. Their blankets had slumped over the side of the bed. Georgie's arm was wrapped around his sister's stomach and when Tabitha drew the blankets up to cover them. The boy shifted and tried to pull himself closer to her, though he was already as close as he could be. Though his grip was firm, Annie didn't seem to be roused by the embrace.

In her bedroom, she checked on the sleeping boy. He hadn't budged an inch. The full color of dawn began to peek through her window, glowing brightly on the deep bruising on the boy's face, which was certainly something to question Mr. Ptolemy about.

Tabitha wrapped a small blanket around her shoulders, revolver in hand, and headed out to the shed. As she approached, she smelled a hint of sweet smoke coming from the shed. The scent all too familiar. She knocked.

"Yes?" came the voice of Ptolemy.

Opening the door, she found the man sitting on a stool, smoking a pipe. He was reading a book by lantern light, his big eyes locking on to her the moment the door was open.

"Morning," he said around the curved stem of the pipe.

"Your boy is still asleep," said Tabitha. "Before I let you in the house, I'd like to know what happened to his face."

Ptolemy slapped the book shut with one hand. "He fell down a flight of stairs at the Black Mustang in Big Spring. That's the short of it. I'm happy to let him tell you the rest, if'n you don't believe me."

She nodded. "I'll be holding on to this," she said, lifting his revolver. "But if you'd like to come in for coffee to ask your questions, now's the time."

The Massacre at Yellow Hill

He rose and set his book upon his bedroll.

She turned, heading back toward the house. "Grab some wood from that pile over there for the stove."

Tabitha had him place the wood inside their iron stove and set it to flame.

He sat at their dinner table, puffing away at his pipe as he watched her grind coffee. "About your husband... Lucas told us something killed him in a mine just outside of town. That the truth?"

Tabitha nodded and poured the grounds into the percolator. "I only learned the truth of it only yesterday from Charlie Gathers, the mine's foreman. He claimed that some kind of creature, unlike anything he'd ever seen, attacked George."

"You know of any reason for these two men to lie to the both of us about what happened?"

"Men lie without needing much of a reason, Mr. Ptolemy, or at least that's been my experience. But it would take an uncommon amount of cruelty for Charlie to tell me and my children that story, if it were a lie. With Lucas telling you the same, I reckon it's the truth, or at least a close version of it. But I've never heard of any creature like what they described."

"I have," he said.

She turned to him, waiting for the water to boil.

"What I tell you now is in strict confidence, Miss Miller—"

"You can call me Tabitha."

He nodded, the blue smoke spilling out of his nose. "Tabitha. The boy in your bed is named Carson. I was once in the employ of his father. He bought me as an extra set of hands and eyes to help him hunt, capture, and study the kinds of creatures that fit the description of what Lucas told me. They are not the only kind of monstrosities in the world, that's to be sure, but they are attached to a group of mad men who, near as I can figure, make their station in Chicago. They call themselves the Society of Prometheus. They worship a malevolent deity from a deranged manuscript, writ in a language that only certain folks can read. Carson's father started off trying to decipher the language, but the writings in that book are poisonous to the mind. They twisted him into madness and ultimately led him down a path that saw him try to sacrifice his own son."

Tabitha covered her mouth as it fell open.

"The Society wants to bring about an event they call 'the Shifting of the Stars.' An elaborate ritual that only one of the Society can perform. Before he died, Mr. Ramos said—"

"He's dead?"

"Indeed, at the hands of a creature known as Sigurd. As he lay dying in Big Spring, he told us that he saw such a manuscript here in Yellow Hill in the possession of—"

"Jeremiah Hart."

"You know him, I take it."

"Hart is the richest man in the county. He owns most property and the mining company that George worked for." She suddenly became flushed with anger. "That son of a bitch had my husband working in a damnable pit for pennies on the dollar. To know that this is what my husband lost his life for..." She swatted fresh tears from her face.

"Carson and I are here to see that his plans do not come to fruition," said Ptolemy. "First thing I plan to do is confront him, take the manuscript, and stop things before they get worse."

"He has an armed group of men who work for him, Mr. Ptolemy. You cannot think to take them on alone."

"But we are alone," came a small soft voice from the hall.

Carson stood in the doorway, rubbing his tired eyes.

The Massacre at Yellow Hill

"Good morning, Carson," Tabitha said, looking over him with a kind of empathetic curiosity. "My name is Tabitha Miller."

"Nice to meet you, ma'am," he said.

The water was boiling, and steam whistled out of the percolator. Tabitha took it off the burner and brought two cups to the table.

"Might I have a cup too, ma'am?" Carson asked as he walked to the table. He wrapped his arms around Mr. Ptolemy's neck. "Sorry I fell asleep in the saddle, Pa."

"You were tired. There's no shame in it."

There was a hard kind of sweetness between the two of them, Tabitha saw. A bond alloyed by loss and mutual survival. She smiled. "You drink coffee, do you, Carson?"

He sat next to Ptolemy. "Yes, ma'am."

She set a third tin cup on the table and poured the steaming black liquid into all three. "We have some sugar," she said, looking back to the counter. She froze, a thin panic flashed through her when she saw she'd left the revolver next to the stove.

Ptolemy put a hand over hers. "There's no need to worry, Tabitha. We aren't liars and we aren't thieves."

She snapped her head around and looked at the man's giant hand over her own, which appeared small and frail compared to his. Nervously, she nodded at him.

"How do you plan to do this thing?" she asked. "With just the two of you against twenty or thirty men?" She walked back over to the stove,

"We've got no intention of taking on Hart's men," Ptolemy said. "None whatsoever."

The boy beside him nodded.

"From what Lucas said, Hart doesn't keep his men on his property. Just at the mine. So, we'll go to Hart's home and judge for ourselves if his mind is too far gone to be reasoned with. One way or another, we'll remove the manuscript from his possession. Then we'll head to the mine, after nightfall to avoid his men entirely. They'll have blasting caps and dynamite at the camp, and we'll use them to seal it shut for all time."

"What's to become of Hart if he refuses to reason with you?" In her heart, she wanted nothing more than for Ptolemy to say that he'd kill Jeremiah where he stood.

"Depends," he said.

"On?"

"How far Hart has delved into the manuscript. If it has fully taken his mind. Carson's father had his eyes on that manuscript every night—every daytime too, near the end of things. Its words change a person. We do not kill lightly, ma'am. We're bounty hunters. Of a certain kind, that's for sure, but we're not murderers. Whether or not Hart lives or dies will revolve entirely around how much the book has changed him and how much he can be reasoned with."

"So, if he hands over the manuscript and lets you destroy the mine, you'll just leave him here to his own devices," she said.

The way that he looked at her with those big penetrating eyes of his told her that he knew the malice in her questioning. "Didn't say that."

"And if he doesn't hand it over, you won't kill him outright?"

"Didn't say that either," Ptolemy said, not a little annoyed with her.

"That man has done enough to the people of this town to merit his own crucifixion," she said. "He buys up all the sources of potential wealth and gives nothing but scrap wages and high rent to those trying to dig out a living in this hellhole. His greed is more than a sin against God, it is a pestilence to us. He took my husband's hopes of providing, and then he took the man himself, all the while staring me in the face and lying to me about what happened." She clenched her fists tight, voice rising. "My children are without a father, Mr. Ptolemy. I'd kill him myself if I thought I might survive and not leave my children without a mother. You want to do some good in this world, by all means take your manuscript and blow his mine to hell and damnation, but do the town an equal good with that gun of yours."

When she finished, she heard the children speaking in their room.

Tabitha straightened the edges of her husband's wool shirt she still wore. Composing herself, she looked at Carson, whose eyes were as wide as silver dollars.

"I will not beg your pardon for yelling in my own home," she said. A tear from each eye tickled at her cheeks. She wiped them away quickly.

Ptolemy puffed at his pipe, his eyes never flinching from the widow's face. The deep lines of his brow furrowed in consideration. "Carson," he said, "go on outside. Give the horses another drink, then saddle them."

"Yes, Pa." Carson crossed the other side of the table. "Thank you for your hospitality, ma'am. Please accept my condolences for your loss." The words so gentle. So sincere.

But before he could exit, Tabitha said, "Carson, wait."

The boy turned back to her, the morning light cutting through the windows casting him in a golden sheen.

She walked over, knelt in front of him, and took him by the shoulders. "You are brave to do what you are doing, and you seem a very good boy." She pulled him close and hugged him tightly. And when she drew back, she saw that he had dropped his chin to hide his blushing face.

"You draw the water, like Mr. Ptolemy said. I'll send Annie out to help you brush down your horses."

When the boy left, Tabitha looked at Ptolemy. "My guess is he hasn't had a mother's embrace in a long time."

"Never has." Ptolemy said. "She died giving birth to him."

She shook her head. "I'm sorry."

Ptolemy stood up. "So am I. The world has been hard on him. Part of me thinks that's why he's able to endure the kind of life we lead. But how much longer he can take it? I don't know."

"If I could—"

"Don't," said Ptolemy. "I know what you're about to say. It will be easy for you to understand that Carson has a gift that our work requires, ma'am. He is tied to a larger worldly fate for me. And he is slowly learning the hard truth, sometimes, God's calling on our life requires deep sacrifice. It is no different for him. And most importantly, and as difficult as it will be for you to understand, though he carries none of my features—he is my son. He does not need saving. He needs protection. Guidance."

The man reached into his back pocket. From a long leather fold, he produced two folded bills, which he slid under his coffee cup. "This should cover our stay for the night and the coffee." He retrieved his gun from the kitchen counter and holstered it.

At the open doorway, he turned back to face her. "I am sorry for the loss of your husband. We come by way of Abilene, through the patronage of a man known as Judge Hezekiah Ellison. If'n you're willing to make your way there, I can assure you that he'd help you make a new life for you and your children."

Tabitha shook her head. "There have been so many promises broken in the life of this family, Mr. Ptolemy…"

"The boy and I don't make promises, Tabitha. Our word is our vow. Make your way to Abilene. Judge Ellison will ensure the rest."

The Massacre at Yellow Hill

Before she could comment further, he stepped out of the house and shut the door.

It wasn't long after when Annie came out of her room with Georgie, their faces still puffy with sleep.

"Who was that, Momma?" Georgie's voice cracked a bit.

"A pair of travelers who needed our help in the night," she said.

She went over to the table and lifted Ptolemy's coffee cup.

Her mouth fell open.

Annie looked at her mother, confused. "What is it?"

Holding two crisp hundred dollar bills in her trembling hand, Tabitha couldn't find the words to answer.

Chapter Twenty-Six

YELLOW HILL, TEXAS

CARSON HAD A tough go of getting water from the pump at first, but once his muscles woke up, he managed to fill the bucket several times over and fill the trough almost halfway.

Ptolemy came around the house, raising his arms high into the air, stretching. Carson watched him pass by without word and walk toward the shed.

"We oughta help her," Carson said as he poured the last bucket of water into the trough.

Hidden in the shed, Ptolemy said, "We're gonna do what we can."

"From what she says, Jeremiah Hart is just as bad as Sigurd or Shirley."

Ptolemy came out of the shed holding two horsehair brushes. "Remind me who it was who told me not a day ago that he was tired of fighting and killing?"

"And who was it who said we do the fighting and killing for a higher reason?"

"Ain't the same."

"Vampires steal the blood out of folks so they can preserve their power and continue on. Why is it we allow men to do it but not them?"

Ptolemy extended one of the brushes to him.

Carson just stared at his father, refusing to take it.

His father pursed his lips, then sighed. "Sigurd and his like are creatures of pure evil. They are crafted from darkness and pain, and they are a perversion to creation. Mankind is no such thing."

"I don't see no difference at all."

Ptolemy's face twisted, angry. "Men like Hart are men, and mankind is made in the image of God. They are afforded mercy and grace, and God wills that each man have his own measure of time to change. No one man is representative of the whole. Hart must be given a chance to see enough goodness in our mercy to allow himself to make the right choice."

Once again, his father extended the brush to Carson. When he didn't take it, Ptolemy dropped it on the ground at his feet and walked over to Vanilla, whose head was still buried in the dark water of the trough.

"Shirking your gelding's needs won't change anything," said Ptolemy as he started to run the comb along the mare's neck. "I've given the widow and her children a chance to make their way to Abilene, where they'll get help from Judge Ellison to make a new life."

"Well, that's nice to do that for them. I didn't know you were going to do that," he said, bending down. He snatched up the brush and made his way to Abraham. After a few brushes down the horse's spine, he said, "What about the rest of the town?"

"Even with as much money as we've made, I don't reckon I can afford to buy a whole town."

"Is that a joke?" Carson's frustration began to boil again.

The Massacre at Yellow Hill

Ptolemy let out a long hard sigh. "No, it ain't a joke. It's a fact. We are helping those we can. Stopping Hart and the society from their dark purpose is our greater gift to the world. What you need to realize is this: it ain't just about finding victory against the society; it's also how we find a victory that matters. Lasts long. If we just go about killing everyone that was put upon by the manuscript, why, we'd be just as guilty as them that are oppressed by it. The evil in this world wounds folks, but that don't mean all that's bent toward evil is beyond mending. They aren't lost forever the moment they lose their way. God requires that we offer a chance at repentance."

"We didn't give a chance to those bandits who came upon us."

Ptolemy thrust his arms over the top of Vanilla and set them to rest there. His head hung low, as if a millstone were tied around his neck. "No, son. We didn't."

"Why?"

Ptolemy's head shot up, his eyes drilling a hole into him. "Because just like with your father, I'd put to death any man who sought to take you from the world. From me."

Now it was Carson's turn to examine the earth at his feet.

"I'll keep telling you that, son. And this: some moments require a kind of violence that is quick and unwavering. This moment with Hart allows us to be prudent. Gives a chance for a man's heart to soften. Every man is like Saul on his way to Damascus. It is of his own folly if he makes choices that end it before he has had a chance to become Paul."

He shook his head. "None of it sounds fair."

"Damn right," his father said. "Neither death nor grace have any bit of fairness to them. That is one of the hardest of life's truths, son."

Before they could continue, quick footsteps came from around the back of the house. He turned and looked.

It was a girl. Her face was purple around her cheek, a long bruise that climb the curve of her face crusted red with little scabs. Her yellow sundress was ringed with a pattern of little white flowers, and auburn curls bounced about her shoulders, swaying in front of her smile. Her eyes were blue and happy, and, in that moment, they became the only thing he could see.

Carson's stomach seemed to stretch and his heart began to pound in his chest. Even more surprising was that she walked directly up to him and threw her arms around his neck, hugging him. She was so warm, he thought. She pressed her lips to his cheek, giving him a kiss.

A kiss that, greater than her warmth, became all he could feel.

She pulled back to look at him, her hands clasped over his bony shoulders. And there, eyes burning in sunlight, their gazes collided.

"Uh," was all he managed.

"Thank you," she said. "Thank you."

"You're welcome?" He craned his head to look at Ptolemy, who continued to brush his horse, a huge grin pulling at his heavy cheeks. "Uh, Pa?"

"Momma told me what the two of you done," she said. "About the money. She said we're going to go to Abilene!"

"I—" He shook his head, feeling stupid. "I'm Carson Ptolemy."

Her lips broke open, revealing a smile that made his heart swell again.

"I'm Annie Miller." She tilted on one foot, peering behind him. "Momma said I'm supposed to help you with your horses. Is this one yours?" She let her hands fall away from his shoulders as she passed him. "He's beautiful! We used to have a horse, but he got old, and Daddy took him out to pasture so he could run free."

Carson turned around, a confused look on his face. "If he was that old, I don't think he let him run—"

The Massacre at Yellow Hill

"That was awful nice of your daddy there, Miss Annie," Ptolemy interrupted, looking at Carson hard in the eyes and shaking his head.

"What are their names?" she asked, running one of her slender hands over the gelding's neck and back.

Abraham chuffed, his skin twitching at her touch.

"This is Vanilla," Ptolemy said, patting the yellow mare on the rump.

"And yours, Carson?" she asked.

The boy squinted at the question. Surprised.

He'd forgotten the name of the horse.

Annie tilted her head and narrowed her eyes, studying Carson.

He remembered, jolting at the shoulders like he'd been hit by lightning. "Abraham!"

She smiled again at him. "You're kinda weird, but that's okay. My friend Orrin is weird too. I don't mind."

Who the hell is Orrin? he thought, suddenly and incomprehensibly jealous at the notion.

Ptolemy joined Annie near Abraham. "You remember how to brush and saddle a horse, Annie?"

"Kinda."

"Tell you what, while I get my things from the shed, I'll let Carson show you how we do it." He smiled at Carson. "It'll be good, for the both of you."

Carson's hands were sweaty, "But—"

"It'll only take a minute," Ptolemy said, as he handed Annie his brush. He turned and made his way back toward the shed.

Still flummoxed, Carson hollered after him, "Where's my brush, Pa?"

Ptolemy didn't turn around. "Still in your hand, son."

"Oh, right," he said, suddenly clutching the brush with surprised fingers.

After working with her for a while, Carson's hands managed to stop shaking. Annie asked him questions about who he was and where he had come from. Over the course of his life, he had learned to lie in these moments to protect himself, but now, with her, he employed none of them. Only the truth passed between them. There was something about how she spoke to him, a kind of bold gentleness, that he had never known.

He asked her about her bruises and the cuts on her face.

"A man attacked me near the saloon," she said openly. "I fought back and killed him. Mr. Gathers took care of the rest and sent me home." She threw Abraham's blue riding blanket over the gelding's back.

Carson turned back toward the shed, making sure Ptolemy wasn't within earshot. "Some moments require a kind of violence that is quick and unwavering. At least, that's what I think."

"It was terrible," she said, her voice drifting away. It was a sound that made Carson sad.

When they finished saddling both horses, Ptolemy walked out of the shed, his saddlebags hanging from one shoulder. "We ready?"

Carson suddenly felt sick to his stomach, realizing that he was about to leave Annie. It hurt to think that he might never see her again. It was an immediate kind of pain, one he did not like at all.

He noticed that Annie looked a little sad too, and for some strange reason that made him feel better. She must have liked talking to him too.

"Annie," said Ptolemy, tying down the saddle bags, "would you run on inside and let your momma know that we're off and tell her that you all should make haste to catch a coach to Sweetwater. From there, y'all can take the train to Abilene."

She looked at him with eyes as blue as the West Texas sky, frozen in indecision.

The Massacre at Yellow Hill

Carson extended his hand. "It was my genuine pleasure to meet you, Annie."

Annie took his hand. Her fingers were so soft, her grip gentle. "It was nice to meet you too. I hope I see you again, Carson."

She turned, smiling, and took off toward the porch.

Carson watched her hair sway like auburn clouds over the yellow wildflowers of her dress. "Me too," he said, though she couldn't hear him.

When she was out of sight, Carson could feel Ptolemy's eyes on his back.

"She's nice." It was all Carson could manage to say about something he could only describe as wonderful. A singular kind of wonderful meant only for him.

"With luck, they'll be in Abilene by the end of the week. Hopefully, one day, we will too. You can check in on her then."

Carson turned to look at his father, who was pulling himself onto Vanilla. "Think she'll remember me?"

"I figure she will," Ptolemy replied. "Got a feeling you won't be forgetting her either."

The boy smiled. "No," he said. "Not a chance."

"Hang on to that feeling, son, and don't be worried. If we succeed today, you'll see her again. Nothing good gets away." Ptolemy smiled at the boy. "Now come on, we've got a wire to post before we deal with this Hart fella."

With their mounts fresh, Carson and his father rode back out to the main road and headed off toward town. He glanced back to see the Millers standing on the porch to bid them farewell.

When Annie lifted her hand to wave goodbye, he made a secret vow to himself, swearing that this wouldn't be the last time he saw her face.

Chapter Twenty-Seven

YELLOW HILL, TEXAS

MR. PTOLEMY AND Carson weren't gone five minutes before Tabitha looked at her children, smiling, and said, "Go pack your clothes. Don't leave anything you'd miss. You won't be seeing it again."

Georgie, excited, rushed inside.

Annie started to follow but then stopped. "Momma," she said, "I'd feel terrible if I didn't at least tell Orrin and his family goodbye."

The idea of Annie going off by herself again twisted Tabitha's stomach into knots. "Annie, I don't—"

"Please, Momma."

Tabitha chewed her lip, considering. It was early morning and the Adolphus family would be eating breakfast.

"Momma?"

"All right, honey, but you go pack your things first. We'll all walk to town together, and while I'm paying the coachman, you can run over there and say your goodbye. But I want it to be quick. No dawdling, you hear?"

"Yes, ma'am," Annie said through a satisfied grin.

In her own room, Tabitha packed everything that mattered to her into two large leatherbound trunks. One trunk was just for her things: dresses, a mirror, a blanket that her mother had knitted for her and George as a wedding present. The other trunk was for George, for though they would be leaving his body behind, his memory would be coming with them in the form of his clothes, revolver, and pocket watch. Tabitha would give them to Georgie when he grew older.

For Annie, she took George's smoking pipe. Annie had loved the smell of her father smoking in the evening time. Also, George's sterling silver cufflinks, which Tabitha had always thought would look fetching if smithed into earrings. They sparkled in her hand as she put them into a leather pouch and tucked them into the trunk.

For herself, she packed George's shirts and his white Stetson hat. Georgie would like that too.

Finally, Tabitha took her white wedding dress from the closet, folded it neatly, and slipped it on top of the rest of the items. For Annie.

As she shut the trunks and latched them, Tabitha couldn't help but notice that her cheeks ached from smiling. It was the first time since George passed that she felt she had a chance to make a life for her children—one they deserved. She didn't know what kind of man Judge Ellison was, but if Mr. Ptolemy's kindness was any kind of indicator, the Millers would fare far better in Abilene than they ever had in Yellow Hill.

She'd once heard from Reverend Callum that there were ranches there. That meant work for Georgie when he was old enough. It would also mean hardworking men who would call on Annie when she was ready to court.

"Y'all packed and ready?" she called from her room.

The Massacre at Yellow Hill

"Yes, ma'am," the children said in unison, then giggled.

"Me, too," she said to herself. "Me, too."

They stacked their luggage on the porch and made their way up the dusty main street toward the center of town. She walked hand-in-hand with Georgie, who asked question after question about where Abilene was, what kind of people lived there, and, most importantly, was Abilene safe.

Tabitha joyfully answered his questions without hesitation.

Just before they reached Carroll Freight and Coach, just north of the Methodist church, she turned to Annie.

"Go tell your goodbyes to Orrin. Make sure to tell him that you'll write him as soon as we get to Abilene. That'll make it easier on him."

Annie nodded then hurried down the walkway. As Tabitha walked toward the coach office, she looked back down the street to see Carson and Mr. Ptolemy riding away from the telegraph station. She waved at them, but they didn't see her to wave back.

They were riding toward Hart's home.

She prayed for their success.

Chapter Twenty-Eight

YELLOW HILL, TEXAS

WIRING JUDGE ELLISON went quickly enough, despite the short bald man who glared at Ptolemy while writing down the message. His beady eyes squinted with disdain for the Black man in his business, but his hand opened quickly enough for Ptolemy's payment.

> IN YELLOW HILL. J.H. HAS MANUSCRIPT, WILL CONFRONT. EXPECT TABITHA MILLER, WIDOW WITH 2. CHARGE ALL EXPENSE TO MY CREDIT. WILL WIRE UPON SUCCESS.
>
> G. PTOLEMY

Back in the saddle, he and the boy rode south to the end of the main street, heading for the three-story home that crowned a large grassy acre of land just outside of town. It reminded him of the homes he'd seen in New Orleans and Mississippi valley, where so many of his kin no longer wore shackles but still lived in the chains of poverty.

He pulled at Vanilla's reins and looked at Carson. The boy was smiling, lost in thought about the girl he met, no doubt.

"Hold up here a minute," he said.

Carson did so and turned his wide eyes on him, listening dutifully.

Ptolemy considered his next words carefully. "I don't know how things are going to play out here, son. I truly don't. My hope is that Hart will not be so far gone as Ezra was, but I can't be sure that is the bent of things. What I can be sure of is that if you see him go for a gun or look like he means us any kind of harm, you must not hesitate to kill him where he stands. He's going to get a chance to help, but we will not give him a chance to do harm."

Carson nodded. "Yes, sir."

"Hopefully it will not come to that. And if, God help us, he manages to hurt or kill me—"

"Pa!"

"No, hear me, son. If he manages that, it will be up to you to find the mine on your own." Ptolemy's eyes screwed into his son. "You find that place and you destroy it. No matter the cost."

The boy's face betrayed his worry.

Ptolemy knew though that Carson was made of stronger stuff than most of the men walking the earth. Why, even before the age of manhood was upon him, the boy had faced down monsters of a dozen kind. The weight of their mission hadn't folded him, and Ptolemy had confidence that when the boy's mettle was tested, time and circumstance would prove it an alloy of wrought iron and holy silver. Strong and pure.

"No matter the cost, Pa, we won't let each other down."

"Or the world."

Carson nodded, the seriousness of a man writ upon face of the child. A brief glimpse of his adult face. "Or the world," he echoed.

The Massacre at Yellow Hill

They trotted their horses up to the hitching post outside the Hart home.

Dismounting, Ptolemy scanned the many windows of the edifice. They shone like mirrors in the morning sun, making it impossible to see inside.

"Eyes wide, ears open," Ptolemy said.

Their boots fell heavy on the whitewashed porch with each step. Ptolemy offered the courtesy of a knock. Then he waited a moment, his hand dangling near the butt of his revolver. When no one came to answer the door, he knocked again, this time pounding his fist on the wood so hard it rattled the glass oval window set in the door's center.

Ptolemy dared to peer through the window, where he spied an enormous foyer that opened up before a flight of steps leading to the second story.

At first, all he saw was the curling banister, but when his eyes carried themselves to the very edge of the window, he discovered a pair of boots sticking through the beveled posts of the landing. One foot was twisted up, the other dangled over the edge of the stairs, the pant leg wet and dripping.

"Ah, hell," Ptolemy said as he took a step back from the door and gave a great kick under the heavy iron knob. The door broke free from the frame with a loud crack, swung on the hinge, and clattered against the wall, shattering the glass into hundreds of shining blades. Ptolemy rushed inside, Carson close behind him, both with their guns drawn.

The rank smell of fresh death swarmed thickly within the house. Ptolemy made his way to the stairs. He put his back to the wall as he climbed them, scanning the banister for where he'd seen the bloody boot.

The second story was as dark as a tomb, the heavy velvet curtains blocking almost all hope of light, but a single undraped window shined a plane light upon a ruin of human flesh lying in the hallway.

A dead man.

Dark blood pooled around what was left of his head, which had been smashed into a horror no longer resembling anything of human likeness. A gun was clutched in his dead fingers, and his trousers were soaked red. The acrid tang of blood and excrement hung heavy.

Carson said, "Is that Har—"

Ptolemy quickly swung his eyes around to his son and put his finger to his lips, shushing him. Shaking his head, he pointed his finger down the dark hallway opposite the dead body.

Carson nodded.

They put their backs to the wall, guns pointed toward the end of the hallway. They went through each room carefully, searching closets and under beds for anyone who might be hiding.

They came to a door unlike anything Ptolemy had ever seen inside a home. It was of heavy iron casting, like what he'd observed inside the banks of large towns.

It was open, though only by a few inches.

Carson tapped Ptolemy on the shoulder and pointed to three small apertures in the wall next to the frame. Whoever the man on the floor was, he hadn't gone down without at least trying to fight.

Ptolemy signed for Carson to take the door by the edge and pull it open.

The boy holstered his gun, grabbed the brass lever at the center of the door, and put all of his weight into swinging it open.

Ptolemy raised his gun, though when the door opened, he saw nothing in the room but a vast library of books encircling a large desk.

No one was inside.

The Massacre at Yellow Hill

He shuffled in and went around the desk. It was scattered with papers and dusty volumes of books. Some of the volumes he could read, others were writ in languages he could have mistaken for half a dozen others. But unmistakable was the large dark outline where the black manuscript had rested. He remembered that the cover left a dark stain on whatever surface it was placed, though neither he nor Ezra had ever determined why. It was as if the book itself were corrosive to anything it touched save the flesh of human hands. The corruption of the volume sunk deeper than skin, burrowing into a man's mind and heart, though it left no trace on the surface.

Carson stood next to the door, his gun in his hand, watching the hallway.

"Believe we're alone," Ptolemy said. "Come here."

Next to the dark stain on the desk, Ptolemy found dozens of sheets of paper bearing chicken-scratch handwriting. Some of the words were of the kind of English he knew, but some of the pages were flooded with the strange symbols Ptolemy had only ever seen in the black manuscript. When he turned back, the boy was still looking in the hallway. Likely at the body.

"Carson."

The boy came over, but before he look at the contents of the desk, Ptolemy said, "The symbols on the pages are the same ones as the manuscript."

Carson inhaled sharply.

Ezra had taught Carson to read the strange symbols, though the boy had only ever read from the manuscript once, per Ezra's instruction. The incident had left him mute for three days and possessed by nightmares for a month.

Only a few weeks after the terror of the reading had passed did Ezra order Carson to read from the manuscript again, but the boy refused. It had thrown Ezra, an otherwise calm and deliberate man, into a fury that left Carson's nose and left eye bloody. Ptolemy had stepped in with intention of beating Ezra to death for hurting the boy who had befriended him, but his intervention snapped the man out of the mania. The next morning, Ezra had apologized to both of them, explaining that he didn't know what had come over him and promising them that it would never happen again.

Only a week later, he'd left Ptolemy for dead, shot through the shoulder and lying face-down in a swamp.

But Ptolemy had proved hard to kill, and he tracked the two of them through the marshes to a place where a great stone obelisk jutted out of a little green island among the dark waters. There, soaked in swamp water and his own blood, Ptolemy found Ezra standing over Carson, the boy's arms and legs tied down and splayed over a kind of stone table in front of the obelisk. Bright green lines of light radiated from the stones, revealing nine stars ascending the stone. The light, somehow, tried to make a coward of Ptolemy. His love for the boy was too great though, and he rushed out of the marsh, one hand clutching his gore-soaked shoulder.

Ezra roared strange words of ritual over the boy, a large skinning knife clutched in his hands. Ptolemy didn't know what the words meant, but formed a kind of harsh understanding to their intent. Perhaps they meant to bring forth something terrible…but perhaps he wasn't. Ezra had known more than Ptolemy knew.

He found his head suddenly swimming with doubt. What if Ezra had been right all along? What if whatever he was bringing into the world was the true right of things? What if—

"Pa!" Carson's voice shattered the daydream.

Ptolemy blinked and found himself clutching one of the sheets of paper that Hart had transcribed. The dark symbols pulsed like throbbing veins.

The Massacre at Yellow Hill

Ptolemy shook his head. "What happened?"

Carson jerked the sheet of paper out of his father's hand. "You started mumbling. Didn't you hear me calling for you?"

"No, Ezra," he said. "I just was trying to…"

No, he thought, not Ezra.

"Carson," the boy said.

Ptolemy rubbed his face to clear his mind. Sweat slathered his hand. "These words are poison, son, and it is even more clear to me now. Even without being able to read them, they have a serious kind of power."

Carson looked at the sheet.

"No," Ptolemy protested.

"We have to know what it says, Pa," said the boy, deciding for himself and for them both.

Ptolemy kept his eyes honed on his son, who scanned the page quickly.

Carson looked up from the page, his pupils shaking, almost as if they were vibrating.

Then, they turned white and rolled back into his head. The boy screamed.

Ptolemy took his son by the shoulders. In between shrill cries, Ptolemy clutched Carson, who began to thrash violently.

"Carson!"

The boy's eyes rolled forward again, his pupils dilated so wide that only the edges were rimmed in green.

"I am the gate!" the boy screamed, slinging spittle into his Ptolemy's face. "I am the key!"

Over and over, he screamed. Sometimes the words came in his own language, and a dozen times over they came in a guttural speech that sunk a stone of fear into Ptolemy's stomach.

"Make passage through this vessel." Carson's throat swelled, his neck straining against some unseen force. "May these stars align. May these stars align." The boy's howls became a keening.

"Carson!"

"That our world might be filled. May these stars align!"

Chapter Twenty-Nine

YELLOW HILL, TEXAS

"**I** DON'T UNDERSTAND," ORRIN said, his face twisted in confusion. "Just like that? You're just gonna leave?"

They stood in the parlor, the boy's arms crossed over his chest, his bottom lip trembling. All Annie's happiness had been overshadowed by the thought that Orrin wouldn't be as happy for her as she was.

"And what happened to your face?" he asked.

Annie sighed. "It's a long story, Orrin, and I promise that I'll tell you. I want to tell you, but Momma says I have to hurry. The coach will be ready soon and... I'm sorry. I'm sorry that I have to go, but I do."

"I'm never going to see you again," he said.

The prospect cut her when she heard him say it. She'd said the same words to herself at night, in bed, when her father had died.

"I'll write you," she said. The promise felt thin, weaker than she had hoped.

"Who am I supposed to be friends with? Who am I going to talk to when you're gone?" Livid, he balled his hands into fists and thrust them by his sides.

Annie just shook her head. She searched her mind for something to say to ease the hurt she could see in his blue eyes, but there was nothing there. So, she wrapped her arms around his shoulders and hugged him tightly. She squeezed him and squeezed him and wouldn't let go.

After a few moments, his hands wrapped around her waist, and he cinched them together at the belly. She felt something warm and wet press against her cheek.

Orrin had kissed her.

Butterflies lifted her stomach into her chest.

She loosened her grip on him and allowed a small space to open between their faces. He kissed her again, this time on the lips. Annie jerked back completely from him, her mouth agape. She saw, with wide eyes, that Orrin's face was wet with tears.

"I—" he said, his mouth fumbling, "I love you."

Annie took a deep breath, unsure.

Orrin's eyes fell to the floor. "I've wanted to tell you lots of times."

Annie tried to stop her head from shaking, tried to say anything in light of this new revelation.

"I told my mother a few times," he said, "but she doesn't understand. She says that it's just because we're friends. But I know that isn't true. I know that I love you, Annie Joy Miller, and I don't want you to go because you're the best friend I'll ever have."

"Orrin," she managed, but nothing came after. When he looked up at her again, the tears were falling down his cheeks like two silver streams.

"Do you love me, too?"

"Orrin, please—"

"Do you?"

"You're my best friend, Orrin. Of course I love you."

The Massacre at Yellow Hill

His brow furrowed, his exposed heart seemed to know what was coming next.

"Just...as friends." His skinny chest sunk, a heavy sigh crawling out of his mouth. "Okay." The word barely above a whisper.

"I'll write, Orrin, I promise. And... and when we're older, you can come to Abilene and stay with us and—"

"Okay," he said, his shoulders beginning to tremble.

"Orrin, please, look at me."

"Please," he said, looking at her as though she'd taken everything from him. "Please write."

"I will. I promise, Slim."

She hugged him again, but this time he gave no return embrace. Over his shoulder, she looked at the clock. The coach would be arriving any moment, and her mother would be worried sick. Though she didn't want to leave her friend in such a state, she couldn't think of putting her mother through another panic.

"Goodbye, Annie Miller," Orrin said.

Turning away from him, leaving him standing in the parlor all alone, she said, "Until I see you again, goodbye, Orrin Adolphus."

Her first steps out of the house were slow, her mind whirling, but as soon as her feet hit the street, she was sprinting. Running from all the hurt she'd endured from this town, but also all the hurt she had inflicted.

She would write and, over time, she told herself, make this right.

Hurrying back toward the coach station, Annie made all kinds of unspoken promises to Orrin, promises afforded only to the very young and the blissfully naive.

She made her way up the walkway toward the coach station. She found Georgie and her mother sitting in the shade on a wooden bench. Her mother was tickling Georgie.

He smiled and giggled. It was a sound Annie hadn't heard for a very long time. Hearing his laugh took some of the pain she had carried with her through the hot dusty street. She sat down next to her mother on the bench.

"The coachman is getting our things at the house," her mother said, leaning in closely as if to tell her a secret. Then she went back to 'getting Georgie's goat,' as she called it.

Saturday in Yellow Hill was alive with morning traffic, dozens of people shuffling down the street on their errands. Annie could hear the blacksmith's hammer clanging like a bell over and over in the air. On the wind, she caught the scent of fresh bread from the baker not two buildings down from them. Across the street, at the general store, she watched a train of miners shuffle inside for various supplies.

Schoolmarm Williams was there too, nodding politely and excusing herself as she moved through the group of dusty miners.

Watching all of these people, Annie saw their lives playing out in front of her like a storybook. A simple story, she thought, but an honest one, and it made her wonder if Yellow Hill had ever been so bad. All the hurt she and her family, even the whole town, had experienced hadn't come through these people, but through Jeremiah Hart.

Can one person really make a whole town seem bad?

It was Hart who had bought up their land when it went bust. It was Hart who made their rent so high and paid her father so little. It was Hart who'd made the poor miners go deep into a cave filled with creatures that Annie's mind couldn't even fathom. Monsters, as it turned out, were real. And they had killed her father.

All these things because one man wanted more and more.

Too much would never be enough for Jeremiah Hart.

Annie's head snapped up suddenly when a giant explosion boomed out from the direction of the mine. A resounding noise like

The Massacre at Yellow Hill

a hundred thunderclaps echoed down the sand flats and set her ears to ringing.

Everyone in the street stopped and turned to look in the direction of the mine, even though it was over two miles away. A knot of worry entangled her heart.

The miners came rushing out of the general store, all of them leaping onto their horses and galloping off toward the sound of the explosion. As they thundered past her, she heard one of the men holler to another, "We ain't supposed to be blasting today!" They were out of sight quickly, a long trail of dust clouding up behind the motley of riders.

Everyone seemed panicked, except her mother, who was smiling. "Seems Mr. Ptolemy and his son have done their work." She looked at Annie. "That sound is them making things right. Only person that should be afraid of that sound is Mr. Hart."

Then, from the direction of the mine, there came a cold, biting wind that ripped through the town. A great thunderhead of clouds rolled forth like black waves swallowing blue sky and golden sun. Then, suddenly there came a flash of light.

Her mother's smile melted into worry. "Come on, kids, we're going to go find our coachman."

Tabitha grabbed Annie and Georgie by the hand. She pulled her children quickly at first, but then broke into a full run back toward the home they'd left behind.

Chapter Thirty

YELLOW HILL, TEXAS

"**S**ON," THE VOICE came from long way away. "Son, please!"

Carson's brain was still on fire, blistered from his interaction with the strange words deciphered from the pages in the study. One moment he'd been reading, the next he was seeing a towering obelisk with bright green lines of gloomy light spilling out of crude symbols carved into the stone. In the vision, a rush of wind blew out of the rockface, so cold it turned the sweat in his hair to frost. Then, the light began to swell like a festering wound until it fissured, pouring open to reveal the aperture of a mineshaft that widened and widened, revealing a wasteland of ice, snow, and…creatures. The things populating the barren waste were so abominable in their anatomy they defied any kind of rational categorization.

Then, he heard the song. The sound of a voice that was not a voice at all, singing. A terrible melody threatening to split the boy's mind.

And over that song came an unmistakable voice.

"Oh, God please!" the voice pleaded. "Please don't go."

Carson stirred awake to find himself clutched in his father's strong arms. Ptolemy was calling his name over and over. It was that sound that buoyed him up out of the darkness and jerked him awake.

"Please stay with me," said the man, who Carson now saw had his eyes shut tight. Begging.

"Pa," said the boy. "I'm here."

Ptolemy's head fell, where it came to rest against Carson's brow. Tears fell from the man's eyes, wetting them both. "Please."

"Pa, it's okay. I'm okay."

"I didn't know—"

"I'm here," said the boy.

The father and son held one another. The man rocking the child back and forth in his strong embrace.

"I saw it," said Carson. "Like before. Like Ezra. Hart found it."

"In the mine?"

"Yes" he said, his mind still dreamy.

Ptolemy nodded, swallowing hard as he steeled himself. "Then that's where we're headed."

The man drew the boy up, where for a moment, he looked upon Carson. Ptolemy ran his palm along the boy's head, smoothing his hair.

"You said I can't leave you, and that means you can't leave me either."

Carson nodded. "We will do it together."

They were out of the house in a dash, mounting their horses and chopping up sand as they galloped east.

It was then that the sky overhead began to cloud over. Huge rolling waves of a dark tempest crowned the firmament of the desert span stretching out before them.

Ptolemy whipped at Vanilla's haunches with the flat of his hand. Carson stood tall in the saddle and rolled his feet in rhythm with his gelding, gripping the reins tight in his fists.

The Massacre at Yellow Hill

Thunder slapped at the air, and blue lightning veined the churning thunderhead. An icy wind blasted them now from the east, so cold it burned Carson's cheeks.

"Over there!" Ptolemy bellowed over the howling wind as he crested a dune. When the boy reached the top, he looked down to see a small encampment. A bonfire burned in the middle of a dozen tents, and a large group of miners stood around it, staring up into the father of all thunderstorms.

A flash of light streaked from the sky and ushered forth a clap of thunder so loud it hit Carson in the chest in a wave of invisible force. Abraham jumped and bucked hard to the left.

Carson clung to the saddle to keep from being unhorsed, and Abraham whinnied in fear.

Ptolemy turned back to make sure Carson was okay.

"Hart is starting the ritual!" Ptolemy yelled over the wind and booming thunder. "We get to the mine, get the dynamite from the camp. Then we'll confront Hart and blow this place to hell!"

Their horses carried them down the tall dune, down among the burlap tents.

They skidded to a stop near the men standing around the fire, who were gawking at the storm like fools instead of taking cover.

One of them turned to see Ptolemy sliding quickly off his mount, and his face twisted in disgust. "Who the fuck is thi—"

Ptolemy jerked his revolver and stuck it in the man's face. "Dynamite. Tell us where it is. Now."

The man's hands shot up into the air. "What the hell?"

The other men were frozen, gazing at Ptolemy and his revolver.

"Hey," one of the miners hollered.

Ptolemy cranked back the hammer of the single action for effect. "I don't have time for your shit. I said, dynamite. Now."

Luckily, only one of the men was armed, the one Ptolemy had chosen to take at gunpoint.

Carson saw the absence of a gunfighter's grit in the man's gaping eyes.

"You only got six shots in that gun," said a buck-toothed man with a rat's nest of blond hair. The man then stepped out of the press of the other miners and drew a long skinning knife from his belt.

Ptolemy reached over to the man in front of him and snatched the miner's revolver free of his gun belt. "I count twelve, shithead," he said.

"Let's rush him," said the buck-toothed man, gesturing at his fellow miners with the blade. "He can't hit all of us."

Ptolemy pointed the stolen revolver at the man and fired. Sparks shot from the blade of the miner's knife as it went flipping out of his hand.

The miner let out a yelp, shaking his hand violently.

"That's eleven. Still enough for the lot of you, and two more for anyone who thinks they're too tough for the first. Now, where's the fucking dynamite?"

"I know where it is," said a dark-haired man with thin lips and bulbous eyes.

"Billy!" the blond man chided him.

"Shut up, Kyle. I ain't getting shot for Hart's sake. I've got a family."

"Carson," said Ptolemy, "go with this man and find us a crate."

―――――――

Carson dismounted and followed Billy, holding him at gunpoint, to one of the nearby tents. The man pulled back a leather tarp, revealing two crates plainly labeled TNT.

The Massacre at Yellow Hill

The cold wind slapped at the tent.

"Please don't kill me," the miner said. His knees shook, and his crotch had turned dark.

"Back to the others," Carson commanded and followed him back to the campfire where Ptolemy stood guard over the miners.

"Is Hart in there?" Ptolemy barked.

"Sure is," Kyle said. "Told us not to let anyone inside."

Back outside, Ptolemy addressed them. "All of you, get on your horses and get the hell out of here."

Nine of the miners ran, heading toward a line of ponies up the hill. The one named Kyle slowly walked backward toward the hill, glowering at Ptolemy.

"If you don't start to run, you're going to find yourself limping up that hill. Now get!"

Kyle took off after the others.

The harsh wind sucked all the moisture out of Carson's mouth when he said, "Over here, Pa." He led his father into the tent with the dynamite.

"Okay, start twisting these fuses together, so as to make one long line we can detonate far away from the camp—"

A howling roar erupted from the throat of the mine.

"Wh-what was that," Carson whispered.

Then came another and another—a harrowing sound of impossible magnitude.

And then another.

Ptolemy shook his head gravely. "I do not know."

Another roar echoed from the mineshaft, sounding closer this time, accompanied by chuffing breaths and snapping jaws. From inside the tent, they could see nothing, but the sounds were unmistakable: a pack of creatures rushing through the camp, howling and yipping.

Then came the screams. The harrowing cries of unarmed miners dying up on the hill.

Carson made for the tent flap, but his father snatched him by the arm so hard it almost pulled his shoulder free of its socket.

He shook his head.

"But—"

Something huge and unseen crashed into their tent, jerking the burlap sheet from its post and partially collapsing the tent.

Carson rolled out of the twisted mass of leather and rope of the collapsed tent. And there, crouched before him, he saw it: as tall as a man at the shoulder, a monstrosity on six legs stalking toward him, growling out of a slobbering mouth made of barbed teeth pronged in a circular snout. Its eyes were green, and scaled black skin covered thick cords of rippling muscle.

Carson went for his gun, but his fingers found only the leather of his empty holster. He dared to move his eyes from the massive predator, searching the ground for his sawed-off shotgun. It leaned its weight onto its forepaws, ready to pounce and swallow him whole.

A volley of gunfire split the air, and bullets drilled into its bristling flesh. The creature howled and turned to look in the direction of the attacker.

Ptolemy stood there, smoking gun in hand, having escaped the burlap skin and snaking ropes. Blood oozed from a long gash in the top of his bald skull. The bounty hunter did not hesitate.

Blam-blam-blam

Three bullets slammed into the wolf's face and shoulder, buckling it. Its skull burst open, the tattered flesh flapping with gore.

But the creature staggered but recovered its balance quickly and bounded toward Ptolemy. The long curved claws sliced through the sand like reaping scythes.

Blam-blam

The Massacre at Yellow Hill

Ptolemy's gun rang out again: this time, the bullets struck the monster in the snout, blowing its nose wide open. Thick black blood splattered into the air.

"Die, goddamn you!" howled Ptolemy.

On the ground, Carson scrambled through the mess of the tent to his shotgun, which still lay amid the wooden posts and ropes.

The revolver cut the air again.

Ptolemy cried out.

Carson whirled to find the creature on top of his father, one razor-sharp claw jutting through the meat of his shoulder.

Rage swallowed him whole. He rushed over to the animal and, as it opened its jaws wide to bite down into his father's neck, he jammed the barrel of his gun into the creature's mouth. Its teeth slashed hot pain through his arm, but he jerked the trigger so that both barrels fired. Hot blood, brains, and fragments of skull sprayed upon the ground.

The creature's feet shot out, its claw ripping free from Ptolemy's shoulder, and it fell on top of him, limp.

"Pa!" said Carson.

"Help me, son," Ptolemy said, trying to heave the creature up off him.

Together, they managed to roll the creature's massive bulk just enough so that he could squirm out from underneath.

"I'm fine," said Ptolemy as he pushed himself to his feet. "Are there any others?"

Carson scanned the camp, his fingers breaking the shotgun open. He reloaded.

When he saw no other of the strange predators among the immediate camp, he looked up to the hill.

"Oh, no."

241

The top of the dune, swirling with sandy powder from the wind, was awash in the blood of the miners and their horses. Though it was growing darker, Carson could see four of the creatures ripping out the intestines of a thrashing horse. It flailed and kicked as it died, screaming.

One of the predators, taller than the others by at least a head, sniffed at the air with a blood-soaked snout. Then it let out a howl. The rest of the pack opened their throats, joining the cry that became an oppressive unison penetrating all other sound.

Thunder exploded above. The clouds were so thick that an unnatural twilight now fell upon them.

Blood ran down his arm, and a large chunk of his shoulder had been torn open so wide that Carson could see the yellow-white bone of the joint.

"You're hurt," the boy said.

"Leave it. I've still got my gun-hand, and that's all I need."

The howling stopped, and the pack began to run.

To Carson's horror, the creatures crested the top of the hill and bolted in the direction of Yellow Hill.

"Annie," he said, and began to frantically look for Abraham.

"The mine, son." Ptolemy clasped him by the shoulder. "Our work is in the mine."

Carson slapped his father's hand away. "But what about the rest of the town?"

"If we don't stop Hart now, it won't just be Yellow Hill that gets ripped to shreds by those things and blown over by this winter storm. It'll be everything and everyone!"

The boy nodded, his guts knotted with worry, but he shuffled through the collapsed burlap tent to gather the dynamite. His father was right, Carson knew, from what he had seen in his vision.

"These are just the first," said Ptolemy. "And if we do what we came here to do, we can make them the last."

Chapter Thirty-One

YELLOW HILL, TEXAS

T HE COACHMAN, A squat man with a bulb for a nose, was loading the last of their luggage on the carriage. Four massive Hackney's chuffed and stamped eagerly at the ground, the chestnut brown hides bristling with the growing storm. The sky had grown dark. A cresting wave of clouds veined with lightning swallowed the horizon of the desert with a winter frost. From the south came a chilled wind that sent goosebumps up Annie's arms and down her spine.

The coachman smiled, his mouth a cavern of jagged, tobacco-stained teeth. "Quite a storm blowin' in, ain't it."

"We need to go!" Tabitha shouted at him as they hurriedly approached.

He tied down the last of their luggage, his bald head shaking. "Uh, no, ma'am. We'll have to wait for that storm to blow past, and seeing as I've got another gent to load up, I don't believe we'd make it out of town in time."

She took the man by the arm roughly, pleading. "Sir, I'll pay you twenty dollars—no, fifty dollars—if it means you get us out of this town right now."

He shook Tabitha's hand from him. "Take your hands from me. I'll lose my job if I leave a paying customer behind."

Her mother looked up to the bench-seat of the carriage and pulled down the short-barreled scattergun perched on the top. Annie gasped.

Tabitha pointed the gun at the coachman. "Mister, you'll lose more than that if you don't get your ass up in that seat and get us out of this godforsaken place."

The man's eyes went wide. "I—I...You can't do this!"

Annie looked at the coachman, then back to her mother. "Momma, what are you doin'?"

"No arguments. Everyone in the carriage, now," she said, thumbing the hammers back on the gun. "Except you." She eyed the coachman harshly.

"There are about half a dozen laws you're breaking right now, lady." The coachman began to back away slowly from the widow with the shotgun.

From the distance came a fresh cry of howls, closer than before.

Tabitha shouldered the shotgun. "There are about half a dozen terrible things coming to this town, and only one of them is that damn storm. Now get your ass up there and drive these horses as fast as they'll go if you want to live."

"Miss, you don't understand—"

Tabitha swung the shotgun around, slamming the butt into the man's face. He fell, twisting to the ground in a heap. The hackneys harnessed to the carriage snorted and stamped furiously.

Annie and Georgie gawked silently. They looked to the groaning man on the ground, then back at their mother. But the woman who

The Massacre at Yellow Hill

Annie saw in that moment looked all at once both like the mother who had raised her and a woman the girl had never seen before, one who was red in the face.

"Get in," said Tabitha. "We're leaving."

They did as she said, scrambling into the carriage, half falling over each other. Their mother slammed the carriage door behind them.

"Lock it," she said, as she climbed up to the driver's bench and took up the horses' reins. She whipped them hard. "Get!" she hollered.

They set off with such a jerk that it sent the children spilling out of the plush velvet seats and onto the coach floor.

The carriage picked up speed, roaring out onto the main thoroughfare.

"Hyah! Goddamn you, horses!" her mother screamed furiously. "Hyah!"

Just past the general store, Annie Miller screamed a name to her mother.

"Momma!" she screamed. "Stop, we have to get Orrin!"

Tabitha Miller whipped the horses again and never looked back.

Annie knelt in the seat and looked out the back window. The rolling storm behind them towered so high and so wide that it blocked the expanse of the wide West Texas sky. As they thundered out of town, she could make out the Hart mansion on the edge of town. Nearby, on the dunes, she thought she could see four strange shapes running. All of them headed for the town.

Chapter Thirty-Two

YELLOW HILL, TEXAS

A CHILLY BLAST SCREAMED from the timber-framed opening of the long, dark mine, so fast and cold it whipped red Carson's exposed flesh. He winced, sucking wind through his teeth, as he rolled a long cable of fuse from a spindle. They'd anchored the line at the mouth of the mine and tied it around a tent peg sunk deep into the earth.

Ptolemy grunted as he carried the crate of dynamite carefully on his unwounded shoulder. The other shoulder poured blood onto his duster sleeve, where it quickly crystallized against the cloth. The wound, sunk deep and split wide, leaked fresh at the joint. Scarlet droplets fell from his fingertips.

Carson didn't know what they would do if they met another pack of beasts. In their current state, they would be unable to fend off just one of those hellacious creatures—and certainly not a whole pack.

The main shaft was easy to follow. The flickering yellow light of oil lamps illuminated the wooden support slats, but not much else. Before them lay darkness.

C.S. Humble

Carson kept his shotgun in his hands, pointed forward. Breathing slowly. Trying to peer into the darkness as far as his sight could go. The shaft became a frozen throat, every whipping gale colder than the last. Teeth chattering, he drew close to Ptolemy, but did not lean against him for fear of tipping him over and making him drop the crate. They were close, but the cold made a gulf too wide for their warmth to touch.

They came upon a place where the wooden slats stopped, and the neck of the shaft opened up into a giant cavern filled with sharp emerald spikes jutting from both ceiling and stony floor. It was there that the fuse line ran out of slack.

"This is as far as it goes, Pa," he said.

Ptolemy set the crate down and then twisted the fuses together to create one long line of cataclysmic intent.

"Let's just blow it up." Carson put his hand on his father's back. "That ought to be enough to stop what's going on in here."

Ptolemy grunted as he pulled himself to his feet using one of the green spikes. "Can't be sure that'll stop what Hart is aiming to do. Destroying the mine is half the job. A job half done, no matter how perilous, is a job not done at all."

Carson looked at his wound. "How bad is it?"

"What, does it look bad?" He forced a smile.

"That's not funny. You promised..."

"I remember my promise, son," said Ptolemy. "And here we are together. I believe there is nothing we can't do if— Wait. Listen!"

From deep within the bowels of the cavern, they heard a voice. A low malevolent chanting.

"Hurry." Ptolemy unholstered his freshly loaded revolver.

They followed the sound to the edge of the cavern wall, where they found another door-size opening. A small stream of water ran from it.

The Massacre at Yellow Hill

This one, though, unlike the timber-framed door of the mine's mouth, had been cut into the stone. From within came a glimmering green light. There were strange symbols carved into the trim of the stone.

Carson knew them. He knew them all too well. He knew their meaning, and, in some way, those symbols knew him.

The chanting grew louder.

They slipped through the door slowly, and Carson was grateful they had when the ground before them suddenly vanished unto a vast chasm as black as a starless night. To their left was a narrow stone bridge leading to the opening of another chamber. Flickering lamplights revealed the slickness of the stone.

Ptolemy stumbled, causing him to slip to one knee, but when the boy tried to take hold of him, he came to his feet again and told Carson that he was fine.

Carson knew he was lying.

They crossed the bridge and came to the chamber door. Two giant statues of indescribable make stood sentinel, their cylindrical heads stretched to the cavern's top. Carson took his eyes away from them quickly; their great height plunged a strange, shameful kind of fear in him. A fear that stole much of the courage he'd built up in the years with Ptolemy. But he followed his adopted father, the large man holding the revolver out before him.

They stepped inside the chamber. The space was shot through with dark green light revealing a slope of stone benches fashioned within the rock formation. From where Carson and his father stood, the benches descended, leading to a central platform. And at the center of the platform was a man.

Lean and gaunt, he stood naked in front of the obelisk that Carson had seen in his vision, chanting. Shimmering radiantly, nine symbols glowed with unnatural, sickening potency like small stars, their coronas blistering with power. Just above the obelisk, there was a great circle of cold light. And in that light, there was a massive, dark shape.

Carson's mouth fell agape when he saw the mass hanging limply against the harsh brightness: a black set of pincers, smooth and slick as a cockroach's carapace attached to a slithering appendage, formed a claw. The claw was bigger than anything Carson had ever dreamed could be attached to a living thing. There came a great groaning sound from far away and as if by some great unseen effort, the writhing appendage pressed through the circle of light, extending. It pushed more of its mass into the cave.

The man chanted, his voice filled with religious ecstasy. His arms thrust up into the air, fingers outstretched.

"Jeremiah Hart!" Ptolemy's voice loud as cannon fire.

The naked man turned. The eyes set within his pale face were bright and wide, filled with mania. "Ah, the first witnesses of the alignment," he howled with religious glee. "Blessed are you, for the first of many gods now breaches the threshold of this forgotten plane! Come and see!"

Ptolemy aimed his revolver at the man.

Hart only smiled. "I see the frost has already touched you, brother! And so you have been baptized in the cold light. Come," he said, gesturing to them. "Bear witness to the first of many titans."

"Shoot him," Carson said, the words surprising even him.

"Hart!" Ptolemy roared. "Stop this now. I've seen this before, and I know you can end it."

The man looked at them, his visage bending into confusion. "Stop? You cannot stop Alitranz or his eight siblings. Their father is the winter cold, the icy touch of infinite space itself. They are the harbingers of the rebirth of the world. Their children are mine to command." He smiled. "I see you have faced them already."

The Massacre at Yellow Hill

"This is your last chance," Ptolemy said, descending the stone walkway toward the thrumming obelisk.

Carson followed, watching as Ptolemy slipped his dripping hand into his duster. The other still clutched his revolver.

"Chance...fate?" asked Hart. "These are the creations of primal man, fool. There is only oblivion and infinity." Hart narrowed his eyes. "If you will not convert, what will save you from Alitranz's wrath?" And Hart gestured to the titan claw above them, which whipped around the cavern. The massive appendage shot forth, heading straight for Carson.

Carson froze, all of his reflexes failing at the sight of the huge claw as it rushed toward him—then Ptolemy was there, pushing him out of the way. The claw slammed into Ptolemy, sending him flying through the air. He collided with the rockface with a sickening, hollow thud and did not rise.

"Pa!" cried Carson, scrambling to his feet.

"The stars are aligned now," Hart said, as the terrible claw swirled and perched itself at the edge of the ever-growing circle of light. He appraised the fallen Ptolemy. "Nothing can stop what is coming. Once this gate reaches its ultimate size, great Alitranz will tear the veil and bring about reckoning. The obelisk is the gate, and I am the key." Hart twisted his grinning insanity toward Carson. "You, boy, I can see your mind. You and I are alike, brothers of the same happy wound. You have seen the wonder and the fury."

Carson looked to his father who lay motionless. "I have." He began to walk toward the howling lunatic, the pillar of light, and the monstrous claw. He lifted his shotgun and leveled it at Hart.

"Killing me won't stop anything! It will only delay mankind's eradication and rebirth. The stars are aligned! The storm has come!"

The priest thrust his hand down in a swooping gesture, commanding the giant claw to fly toward Carson again. This time he ducked and rolled forward, tucking the shotgun across his waist. When he came up, he pressed the barrels directly into Hart's naked chest.

The man looked down at him, still smiling that insane grin. "Choose now, boy. Choose a better world."

Carson chose.

He squeezed the trigger.

The blast boomed in the cavern and a red mass opened upon Hart's chest, spraying the wall behind him with a thick welter of gore.

The gaunt man twisted violently and fell to the ground. Silent and unmoving.

The great claw raised high, and a wailing roar ushered forth in the cavern so loud it drove Carson to his knees. His eardrums splitting, he ducked again as the claw smashed at the cavern walls.

The tendril extended in length, the mass of its dark shape swelling even greater into sight. Alitranz was closer. Alitranz would come through. The cold permeating from its darkness would frost every landscape, still all waters to glass.

They were too late. They had failed, and now all they could do was run.

Carson ran to Ptolemy, ducking low as the tendril wildly whipped around him, carving through the stone seating and smashing into the cavern walls.

"Pa," Carson cried. "Pa, get up!"

Ptolemy's eyes fluttered open. He reached up to caress his son's face. "Are you all right?"

"Come on, we have to get out of here."

The Massacre at Yellow Hill

"I'm all broken inside, Carson. But if you can get to me over to that stone," he said, producing a single stick of dynamite from his jacket. "I can stop it."

Inside Carson's heart, a pillar tipped over. "No," he said.

"Help me, boy. Help me do the thing we were put on this earth to do."

Tears filled Carson's eyes, and he shook his head. "I won't leave you here!"

The great claw smashed into the wall above them, shattering rocks all about them.

Carson wept, throwing himself against the man he loved. "I don't want to be without you. Please don't leave me."

Ptolemy laid his arm across the boy, holding him. "It's you that's gotta leave me. I don't know what the world holds for you, but I know that you've got further work to do. And that work is for you alone. Now, help me lean into my purpose."

Carson, tears streaming down his face, clutched his father close and hugged his neck fiercely. "I love you so much, Pa."

"I love you too, son."

Underneath a wailing titan, Carson dragged his father. The man was heavy and his clothing was slick with blood, but the boy's grip and strength proved true. The claw battered the cavern walls all around them, sending stones raining down around the bounty hunters. Finally, with almost all his strength exhausted, Carson pulled Ptolemy over to the blistering light of the obelisk, groaning with all his effort.

"Take these," Ptolemy said, handing Carson his revolver. Wrapped around the sandalwood grip was the chain and flat medallion face of his father's pocket watch. "Never forget mercy, son. Act justly. Be upright. Do good."

Carson took the revolver and watch, his face wet with tears and blood. "I...can't do this without you."

"You can. You will. Go to Abilene. Meet with the Judge," said Ptolemy. "And take care of that girl and her family. Now, go, I don't have much breath left, and you have to get clear of what's coming."

Carson hesitated, tears falling. "I love you, pa."

Ptolemy took his son's face in his hands one last time. "I love you, Carson Ptolemy. Always and forever."

Carson, unable to speak, kissed his father on his wounded brow and then turned to run.

He turned back to look at his father one last time at the top of the cavern steps. But what he saw instead was the great gaping hole of green light, the gateway revealing the terrible face of something ancient and unknowable.

"Go, son!" The last command of his father.

Carson obeyed, hurrying, panting wildly as he slipped along the thin bridge over the chasm. He slipped his father's revolver into his belt and pounded back through the shaking cavern.

It was only when he reached the edge of the mine that he heard a great explosion from deep within the earth.

The ground shook.

He ran and ran until he reached the exit. The howling wind of the winter cold cut about his face as he broke open one of his shotgun cartridges and poured the gunpowder along the starting length of the fuse.

"Whatever the cost," he said as he struck a thick match against the exterior wall of the mine shaft. The fuse took to the match, the gunpowder giving a tiny whoosh as the flickering flame streaked down the length of the mine.

The Massacre at Yellow Hill

He turned to run when, just off to his right, he spied Abraham and Vanilla taking refuge from the cold wind under a single fruitless mulberry tree. He hurried to them, took Vanilla's reins into his hands, and wrenched himself atop Abraham.

He rode to the top of the dune with the horses. He pulled Vanilla close to Abraham, so they stood shoulder-to-shoulder, and wrapped his arms around neck of both the mare and the gelding. He clutched them tight until the boom of the detonation rumbled the ground beneath their feet. Both horses jumped and skittered, but he kept them close, shushing them to calm. The force from the explosion blew boulders, pebbles, and dust out of the mouth of the mine.

Astride Abraham, he looked back at the sunken pile, and his heart broke. Carson had now buried a second father in a single lifetime.

He rode back to town, passing crumpled body after body. Dark blood flowing from the corpses had matted the thirsty yellow grass and dry sand. The bodies were men, women and children, all strewn about the streets, their clothes shorn open and their flesh riven the same.

He made his way to the Millers' home. There, he knocked on the door, but no one answered. He stepped inside to see if he could find anyone, but he was happy to find it empty.

Next, he went to the general store. The place was an utter ruin, filled with bodies torn asunder. Skulls slashed through. Limbs strewn about, resting in dark pools of blood slathered about the floor.

You cannot stop it... you can only delay, Hart had said.

Carson, remembering the howling ravings of Hart, picked up a canister of kerosene from inside the store transformed into a slaughterhouse. He took it and rode back to the Hart mansion.

He hitched the horses outside before dousing the porch and foyer. Then he drenched the whole of Hart's dark study with the acrid liquid.

After it caught flame, he took Abraham and Vanilla by the reins and led them a short distance away.

And he watched from the three-story monolith burn.

Riding through the sandy, crimson streets, Carson set his course toward Sweetwater. There, he'd wire Judge Ellison, only reporting that he was on his way, and that Ptolemy hadn't survived.

He'd wait until he was there in person to tell the Judge of what was coming, of what great mission now was beset upon him.

Carson didn't know if Hart had been telling the truth, that they could only delay the end of all things. Only time would tell.

Shivering against the wind, he rummaged through the saddle bags, looking for a blanket. There, rolled up within one of the bags, was Ptolemy's winter coat given to him by Ezra in the years before… before all this. Trotting through a newly frozen desert waste, feeling more alone than perhaps any person had ever felt before, Carson wrapped himself in his father's coat.

It kept the cold at bay as best it could.

CEMETERY DANCE
PUBLICATIONS

We hope you enjoyed your
Cemetery Dance Paperback!
Share pictures of them online, and tag us!

Instagram: @cemeterydancepub
Twitter: @CemeteryEbook
TikTok: @cemeterydancepub
www.facebook.com/CDebookpaperbacks

Use the following tags!

#horrorbook #horror #horrorbooks
#bookstagram #horrorbookstagram
#horrorpaperbacks #horrorreads
#bookstagrammer #horrorcommunity
#cemeterydancepublications

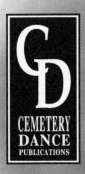

CEMETERY
DANCE
PUBLICATIONS

SHARE THE HORROR!

Printed in France by Amazon
Brétigny-sur-Orge, FR

21025684R00150